The Extraordinarily *life of*

Cassandra Jones

Walker Wildcats Year 1: Age 10

The Extraordinarily Ordinary Life of Cassandra Jones
Walker Wildcats Year 1

Tamara Hart Heiner

Print edition
copyright 2015 Tamara Hart Heiner
cover art by Octagon Lab
Illustrations by Elisa Allan

Also by Tamara Hart Heiner:
Perilous (WiDo Publishing 2010)
Altercation (WiDo Publishing 2012)
Deliverer (Tamark Books 2014)

Inevitable (Tamark Books 2013)
Lay Me Down (Tamark Books 2016)

Tornado Warning (Dancing Lemur Press 2014)

TABLE OF CONTENTS

Episode 1: The New Girl

CHAPTER ONE

New School

The van door slid shut behind Cassandra Jones as her brother climbed out, and still she stood in front of the new school, staring up at it. Her heart thumped out a staccato rhythm at double time. *Duh-dum, duh-dum, duh-dum.* She knew where her classroom was; her mom had shown her when they visited the school a few days ago. No, that wasn't the problem.

The problem was, she didn't know anyone. Last year had been the best one ever at North Ridge Elementary. She spent every spare moment with her best friend, Tammy. Her mind flashed on those images now, eating lunch together, running on the playground, trying to see who could go the highest on the swing set at Tammy's house.

They'd left Texas right after the last day of school. As in, Cassandra walked out the school doors, talking with Tammy, and saw her mom's van waiting in the pick up line. The whole family was already inside, the vehicle packed to the rafters with everything the moving truck hadn't taken.

And in that moment, the gravity of the situation hit Cassandra like a grand piano. She thrust her arms around Tammy and sobbed into her shoulder.

"Cassie. Cassie!"

Her mom's voice behind her made Cassandra zone back into reality. She blinked back moisture and turned to the open window and the van that hadn't moved.

"Cassandra, I'm holding up the line," her mom said, weary lines etched around her eyes. Still, she pursed her lips together, and Cassandra knew her mother wasn't unsympathetic to her plight. "You've got to go inside, Cassie. You're going to be fine."

Cassandra nodded and forced her feet to step forward. Her younger brother and sister were already gone, fearless in the face of the unknown. They just didn't know enough to be scared. Cassie did. She was a fifth grader now, and she knew how mean kids could be. She'd had a good group of friends in Texas, solid protection. She had nothing here.

Being late wasn't the first impression she wanted to make, either. She quickened her pace and ducked into the classroom, depositing her lunch box next to the others lined up against the wall. She found the desk Ms. Dawson had showed her last week and settled into it. Cassandra kept her eyes down while surveying her new classmates out of the corner of her eye. A boy with brown hair and glasses chatted with another boy, and a girl with short, reddish-blond hair showed off her new folders to a larger brunette. A few glanced her way, but most paid her no mind.

Cassie felt the breath slide out of her, and some of the tension worked its way out of her shoulders. This couldn't be that bad, then. Nobody laughed at her or pointed her out as the new girl.

The eight o'clock bell rang, and the teacher started the class. She called roll. Cassandra tried to pay attention to the names, but they passed by in a blur. She remembered to call out "Here" when Ms. Dawson read, "Cassandra Jones."

"Sometimes I go by Cassie." The sentence was at the tip of her tongue, but she delayed too long and was too timid, and Ms. Dawson had already moved on.

Ms. Dawson gave out orders to organize their school supplies before copying down the sentences on the board. Copying sentences. This was familiar and easy, if not boring. The class worked in silence, and Cassie didn't have to worry about whether anyone would speak to her.

"All right, it's time for morning recess," the teacher said, and Cassie's traitorous heart started to gallop again. Would anyone play with her? Would she be left alone at the sidewalk?

"Let's line up alphabetically." Ms. Dawson read out their names, and each child stood in turn and lined up at the door. "Matthew Higgins. Riley Isabel. Cassandra Jones."

Cassandra stood, smoothing down the skirt of her first-day-of-school dress. She never wore dresses except Sundays and the first day of school. In fact, until recently she had considered herself a tomboy, happier up in a tree than with a doll. But she'd felt a secret thrill of pleasure when her mother removed the curlers this morning and Cassandra caught a glimpse of her reflection, red pleated dress and full curls tumbling down her back. She looked pretty.

The girl with the short strawberry-blond hair was in front of her. She cast a glance back at Cassie and faced the front again. Cassie wanted to say hi, but the thought of speaking out loud when no one had called on her made her throat go dry. Instead she planned what she would say the next time the girl turned around.

They marched down the hall in a semi-straight line, some kids dragging their feet or walking slightly out of sync with the rest. As soon as they burst through the back doors to the play yard, however, the line dissolved. Children filtered out like ants from a scattered anthill. It was a large play yard, with a soccer field on one side, swings, tether balls, monkey bars, and a metal dome climber in the middle, and trees on the other side.

"Wow," Cassie said, speaking in spite of herself. "It's so big."

"There's more on the other side," Matthew said, still standing close to her. "This is the upper grades playground." He looked at her and then turned away, his cheeks coloring. He dashed off the sidewalk and joined the other kids.

Cassie smiled. She wasn't an outsider, then. Someone had spoken to her.

She didn't join in with the other girls. She didn't know them well enough. Instead Cassie went to the swings. She pumped her legs and went as high as she could. Up here, with the wind streaking through her hair and around her ears, no one else existed. It didn't really matter if she knew anyone or had friends.

Ms. Dawson blew her whistle, and kids withdrew from different areas of the play yard, regrouping as if sucked in by a magnet. "Line up in order!" she shouted.

Cassie looked around for the short-haired girl. She waited until the other girl had stepped into line, and then Cassie got in behind her. "Hi," she said, gathering up her courage.

The girl didn't even turn around. Maybe she hadn't heard.

They cleaned up after recess and did some book work before going to lunch. Kids with lunch boxes lined up on one side, and those buying lunch lined up on the other. Cassie noted with relief that meant she wouldn't have to be next to the short-haired girl.

She didn't have the chance to wonder who would sit by her, either. They filed into the cafeteria and sat down at their table in the same order they'd been in line. Cassie opened up her blue lunch box, wondering if her mom had remembered that she didn't like peanut butter and jelly sandwiches.

Someone tapped her on the shoulder. "Cassandra?"

She looked up, trying to hide her surprise.

The brunette from her class stood there. She brushed her shoulder-length hair back, balancing her lunch tray on her hip. "Want to come and eat lunch with me?"

Cassie looked toward the table by the windows where she pointed, with another teacher and several other kids. "Am I allowed to do that?"

The brunette smiled, showing colorful elastic bands around the braces on her teeth. "Yep."

"Sure." Cassie packed her lunch back up and followed the other girl. She tried to contain her joy, but she felt as if she'd won a prize. Someone she didn't know wanted to eat lunch with her.

"I'm Danelle," the girl said as they sat down with the other students.

"And I'm Ms. Buckley," the teacher said. She had short blond hair and tiny wrinkles around her eyes. She smiled at Danelle. "I'm the school counselor."

"Hi," Cassie said, unwrapping her peanut butter and jelly sandwich. Great. "I'm Cassandra. You can call me Cassie."

The other kids introduced themselves, and Cassie realized half of them were new, also. Cassie nodded at them and put her sandwich aside for the other food offerings in her box. Grapes, chips, thermos of milk.

"You don't like your sandwich?" Danelle asked.

Cassie shook her head. "Not really."

"Here, trade with me." Not even asking, Danelle swapped out Cassie's sandwich for her chicken fingers. "It's my favorite."

"Thanks," Cassie said, staring in wonder at her. What would it be like to have that kind of confidence? To be so sure of herself and others around her?

"So where did you move from?" Danelle asked, biting into the soft white bread and speaking around the food.

"Texas," Cassie said, warming to the subject. "I loved it there. I miss all my friends. But my dad, he got a job transfer. So now we're here."

"In Arkansas," Danelle said, taking a swallow of milk.

Cassie nodded, feeling her smile slip a bit. "Yeah."

"What do you think of it so far?" Ms. Buckley asked.

She hesitated in her response. She hated it here, and they'd only lived here three months. She hated the small apartment that passed for their house, hated that all her friends were still in Texas, hated the snakes and spiders she spotted anytime she walked outside.

But she knew she couldn't say that. "The people are nice," she said. She tacked a big smile on to the end of the sentence, hoping Ms. Buckley would buy it.

"That's right," Danelle said, nodding. "The nicest people ever here."

<hr />

Turned out that Danelle's last name was Pierce, and she was two people behind Cassie at line up.

"Hi," she said to Cassie when they lined up for afternoon recess.

"Hi," Cassie said back, grinning. They met up again outside.

"Do you like to swing?" Danelle asked.

"My most favorite thing!" Cassie replied. They raced to the swings, each girl pushing harder to make hers go the highest.

When Ms. Dawson blew her whistle, Danelle jumped off without even stopping her swing. "Come on, Cassandra!"

Cassie hesitated. Tammy had told her horror stories about people jumping off of swings and cracking their heads open. She'd always been too afraid to try.

"Silly goose!" Danelle said. "We have to line up!"

Cassie tucked her legs under her before thinking maybe that wasn't such a good idea. Instead she straightened them, took a deep breath, and jumped off. The momentum flung her forward, and her legs struggled to keep up. She stumbled through the grass until Danelle grabbed her arm, laughing.

"I can tell you haven't done that before," she said.

"Yeah," Cassie agreed.

"You'll have plenty of chances to practice." She raced on ahead, and Cassie followed, breathless.

♥

Today, and today only, Cassie's mom waited for them in the car line. Tomorrow they would all ride the bus to the apartment in Fayetteville. The idea rather excited her. She'd never been on a bus before except for field trips.

She found her brother and sister, Scott and Emily, waiting outside with the mobs of students. "How was school?" she asked them.

"Great," Emily said, and she launched into a lengthy description of the classroom rules and what activities they had done. Cassie tuned her out. She hadn't really wanted a play-by-play.

"Scott?" she asked.

"Boring," he replied.

"You're in first grade!" Cassie said. "How can it be boring?"

He shrugged.

Cassie waited for someone to ask her, but no one did. So she stated, "Well, my day was great. I've already made a new best friend." She waited for a reaction, but Emily and Scott just stared at her. Cassie let out a dramatic sigh. "Don't you get it? If you don't have a best friend, you don't have anyone to hang out with. No one to tell your secrets to. No one to celebrate with you when you do great. No one to play with at recess. Having a best friend is the most important part of school!"

Emily's face lit up, and Cassie knew she'd caught on. "Yeah! I made a best friend."

"Not me," Scott grumbled. "I didn't make any friends."

"Bye, Emily!" someone called. All three of them swiveled to view a girl with long blond hair and big blue glasses waving as she got into a car.

"Bye!" Emily called back, waving emphatically. "See you tomorrow!"

"That your new best friend?" Cassie asked.

"No. I can't remember her name. My new best friend is Alyssa. She sits by me."

"Ah," Cassie said. "My best friend is. . . ." Her words trailed off as she took stock of the waiting area. Only about five kids still lingered around the curb, but there were no more cars in line. "Where's Mom?"

A teacher came out of the school, a slight frown crinkling her forehead. "All right, everyone inside. We'll start calling parents in a few minutes."

"Were we supposed to ride the bus?" Emily said, her brown eyes wide and fearful. "Maybe Mom's at home waiting for us!"

"No, we weren't!" Cassie snapped, her sudden worry making her cross. Her head pounded with an oncoming headache. Mom wouldn't forget them, would she? She never had before. At their old school, they would walk several blocks and meet up with the car. Had she expected them to walk? Cassie shook her head. Couldn't be. She wouldn't even know which direction to go.

They trooped into the hallway between the entrance and the office. The other kids sat down on their backpacks or rested their heads on them, all looking tired and defeated.

"Where's your mom?" Scott asked a little boy.

He gave a shrug. "She'll be here. She's always late."

"Late," Scott echoed, as if tasting the word.

Cassie squeezed her fists together and stared out the window, willing the blue van to appear. Any moment now, her mom would come into view, apologizing for whatever had kept her from being here on time.

A yellow car slid against the curb, and the little boy jumped up and ran outside.

The teacher came into view again. "Okay, let's start calling parents." She pointed at Cassie. "We'll start with you."

Cassie stared at the teacher, her mouth suddenly going dry. She'd just remembered something. She didn't know their new phone number.

CHAPTER TWO

Misunderstandings

Cassie followed the teacher into the office, squeezing her hands together as she went. The woman picked up the phone and handed it to Cassie. "Um, it's just," Cassie whispered.

"What?" The woman leaned closer. "I couldn't hear you."

"I don't know my phone number," she whispered.

The teacher sighed and put the phone down. She went behind the desk and opened up a filing cabinet. "What's your last name?"

"Jones."

She thumbed through and stopped on one. "First name?"

"Cassandra."

The thumbing resumed until she found what she wanted. She pulled it from the cabinet and picked up the phone. "Is this a cell phone or a landline?" she asked, punching the numbers into the phone.

"Landline," Cassie answered.

The woman handed the phone to Cassie. She pressed it to her ear, listening to the monotone ring. Then it stopped, and her mother's voice on the machine picked up.

"You've reached the Jones's. Leave us a message, and we'll get back to you as soon as we can!"

She hung up before the beep and shook her head. "No answer."

"Well, she must be on her way here." The teacher didn't look too pleased. She ushered Cassie back into the hallway and disappeared into the office with another student.

"Did you reach Mom?" Emily asked, chewing on her fingernails.

Cassie looked down at her own nails. She'd broken the chewing habit just this summer, but she had the urge to start up again. "No. She's probably almost here."

The words were barely out of her mouth when the blue van pulled into the parking lot, coming to a hasty stop at the curb in front of the doors. Emily and Scott bolted from the hallway. Cassie followed behind, her relief morphing into anger. First day of school. How could she do that to them?

She climbed into the front seat and settled her backpack on the floor as Emily blabbed away about what a great first day it had been. Putting on her seatbelt, Cassie interrupted. "What happened? Was there a car accident? An emergency."

Her mother shot her a weary look. "No, Cassandra. No emergency. I'm very sorry I'm late."

And that was it? No further explanation? Cassie wasn't

ready to let it go. "First day of school, Mom. And you weren't there." She didn't feel like talking about the way the teacher had looked at them, the way it felt to be forgotten with the other kids who expected to be forgotten. "Why weren't you there?"

Her mom pressed her lips together. "We live farther away than I thought. It won't happen again. From now on, you're on the bus."

Cassie leaned her head back and released a sigh. That was something, at least.

"What about you?" her mom said, attempting conversation. "How was school?"

Cassie shrugged. "Fine. It was fine."

They pulled away from the curb, but didn't head the direction Cassie expected. "Where are we going?" she asked.

"To the new house." Her mom gave her a smile. "We should have everything ready to move in this weekend."

"Really?" Cassie gasped.

"Yay!" Emily cheered in the back. Even Scott looked excited, and nothing excited him. Anette didn't look up from her dolls. She probably didn't care.

They took back roads out to the countryside. No wonder her mom hadn't been on time. Cassie looked at the plantation-style house, more anxious than ever to move into it. The two-bedroom apartment they were staying in was way too crowded for the six of them. She wanted her space back.

Mr. Jones's small green sports car was already parked in

the driveway, a large white moving van in the circle drive. He greeted Mrs. Jones with a kiss, and then the kids exploded out of the van, heading for the house.

"Grab a box," he shouted, gesturing to the moving truck. "Don't go in empty-handed."

"But we don't know where things go," Cassie said.

"Just put it inside somewhere."

They trudged back and Cassie picked up a smaller box labeled "kitchen." Okay, so maybe she could figure out where this one went. She pushed open the front door, walking through the tiled entryway and to the kitchen. Both tables had already been set up. She put the box on the dining room table and headed for the bedroom she shared with Emily.

She sighed in contentment. It wasn't a big room, but it would just be the two of them, instead of all four like it was now. The bunk bed was already set up. Cassie pulled open the accordion doors that shielded the closet. There was a bookshelf for her books. Suddenly she wanted to get all those boxes into the house. She couldn't wait to start unpacking and make this place hers.

♥

It didn't take long to settle into a routine at school. Each day remained relatively predictable. Cassie had Danelle, and the comfort of having a good friend took away the unease she had at other new activities.

By the end of the weekend, the Jones were mostly settled in their new home. Mr. Jones surprised the family with a dog and cat from the local animal shelter to christen the house. The kids were delighted and named the cat Baby Blue, because she was a Siamese with big blue eyes. The dog they named Pioneer. Cassie wasn't sure her mother was as delighted.

This Tuesday Cassie was especially excited, because it would be her first Girls' Club meeting. She'd been a part of the same unit for four years in Texas. One of the first things her mom had done was sign her up here.

Ms. Dawson handed out little blue books to everyone. Cassie opened hers up. It only had one page inside: a white sheet with twenty blank squares centered around an ice-cream cone.

"What is this?" Emmett Schrimmer asked.

"This is your reading log," she said, stepping to the front of the class and smiling at everyone. "When you finish reading a book, you come and tell me, and I'll give you a sticker. Put it in one of the squares. It has to be a chapter book, not a picture book. Once you have all your squares filled in, I'll take you out for an ice-cream cone."

This announcement was met by cheers and excited chatter from the students. Cassie grinned. Twenty books. She could get that done in a month.

⟨✦⟩

"Clear your desks and put your books away," Ms. Dawson said. "Then everyone line up."

Cassie glanced at the time. Morning recess. She got in line behind Riley, the blond who never said a word to her. Cassie turned around and smiled at Danelle, who winked at her.

"Let's go!" Ms. Dawson said.

Cassie started after Riley and nearly tripped. Glancing down, she saw her shoelace was untied. She stepped out of line to tie it, pausing to tighten up the other one, too.

The class continued without her. When she looked up, everyone had gone, including Ms. Dawson.

Cassandra jumped to her feet, anxious to catch up with her class before anyone noticed she was missing. She knew her way to the play yard, at least. She headed that direction, folding her arms in the hall so no one would question why she was out by herself. She marched so that her ponytail swung like a pendulum. Her shadow on the walls entertained her until she got outside.

The first place she headed was the swings. Cassie let herself ride higher and higher into the wind, enjoying the exhilarating feel of freedom that accompanied her. In a moment, she knew Danelle would notice her and come and join her. Until then, she'd just pump as hard as she could. Her eyes swept the play yard, trying to locate her friend with the shoulder-length brown hair. She didn't spot her. She slowed her swinging a bit as she turned to search the soccer field, just in case Danelle had decided to play.

For that matter, she didn't see anyone she recognized.

Cassie's momentum stopped as a feeling of trepidation crept through her chest. She hopped off the swings and ran over to the monkey bars. She climbed along with the other kids, feigning calmness, all the while looking for a familiar face, another classmate. She jumped down and made her way to the other side of the play yard, checking the younger grades' playground just in case.

Her class wasn't here. Cassie was sure of it now.

Maybe they'd gone back to the room. Maybe Ms. Dawson decided to do indoor recess today just for a change.

No one objected when she hurried back into the building. Her heart pounded in her throat, and she could just imagine the trouble she'd be in for losing her class.

The classroom door was open, and she took a deep breath before stepping inside.

No one. The room was empty.

Cassie stood there, blinking back tears. Now what? She was all alone and had no idea where to go.

CHAPTER THREE
Club Girls

It was time to ask for help. Cassie knew where to ask, but the very thought made her knees weak. She needed to walk into Ms. Wade's class and tell her she was lost. Ms. Wade would fix this. But first, Cassie needed to gather all of her courage. She wiped her eyes and prepped herself with several deep breaths. Then she walked across the hall.

The door was closed, and she hesitated. Should she knock? Or just walk in? She opted for a brief knock before pushing the door open.

Ms. Wade turned from the blackboard and looked at her expectantly. "Yes?"

Cassie focused on the teacher, ignoring the curious staring eyes that latched onto her. She walked over and whispered, "I've lost my class."

Ms. Wade blinked, her expression bewildered, and then it melted into what Cassie hoped was sympathy. "Come on. I'll help you find them." She looked at her students. "I'll be gone for a few minutes. Work on your reading assignment. Monica, take names. If anyone talks or makes noises, let me know."

"Ms. Dawson's your teacher?" Ms. Wade asked as she led Cassie from the room.

Cassie nodded. "We always have recess right now. But I went out there and no one's there."

"Hmm," was Ms. Wade's non-committal reply. She didn't say anything else as they trooped through the school. "Wait here," she said, stopping outside a room.

Ms. Wade disappeared inside, and Cassie waited. She read the plaque next to the door. "Teacher's Lounge." So this was a room just for teachers. Was Ms. Dawson here? Where was her class, then?

Ms. Wade emerged with Ms. Dawson, who looked Cassie over with bewilderment.

"I'll be going now," Ms. Wade said with a wave.

"Thank you," Ms. Dawson replied, and then focused on Cassie, staring down the bridge of her nose at her. "Why aren't you with the class?"

Cassie swallowed and blinked quickly to discourage the gathering tears. "I stopped to tie my shoe. When I looked up, everyone was gone. I thought they went to recess, so I went too. But no one was there." The treacherous tears were forming in her eyes, in spite of Cassie's best efforts. Suddenly she longed for her old school. She longed for the familiarity of the routine, the hallways, the teachers she knew, the classmates she'd grown up with for years. This school wasn't her place.

Ms. Dawson put a hand on her shoulder. "It's all right. The class is at P.E. We have morning recess every day during the first week of school. After that, we only have it on Mondays. The rest of the week, it's P.E."

"Oh," Cassie said dumbly. What an idiot she'd been to assume she knew the schedule around here. "Where's P.E.?"

"In the cafeteria. Come on, I'll walk you there."

Cassie would rather not go. She didn't want to show up for a class fifteen minutes late and have everyone wonder what happened to her. But she certainly couldn't tell Ms. Dawson no. She trudged along behind, no longer excited about anything this day had to offer.

Cassie walked into the cafeteria timidly. She didn't expect anyone except Danelle to notice she was missing, but several of her classmates spotted her.

"Where did you go?" Karla asked. "You just vanished."

"Cassie!" Danelle gave her a hug. "Did you get sick?"

"I got lost," Cassie said, going for the humble pie. "I thought you guys were at recess."

That earned some polite titters from her classmates, but nobody was rude. In fact, everyone was super nice about it, as if they understood how traumatizing that was for the new girl.

Maybe it's not so bad here, she thought. *Maybe I need to give it more time.*

"Remember, Cassie, you're not a bus rider today," Ms. Dawson said that afternoon as Cassie put her homework in her backpack. "Your mom sent a note. You've got Girls' Club after school."

"Thank you, Ms. Dawson," Cassie said. She hadn't forgotten, of course. How could she? Her stomach was in knots again at the thought of meeting her new unit. She'd been a part of her old troop for five years, starting in Kindergarten. She had been closer to those girls than anyone else at school besides Tammy. Had this unit been together just as long? She'd be the odd girl, the intruder.

The final bell rang. Cassie put on her backpack and picked up her lunch box before making her way to the cafeteria.

She spotted the group immediately. A lunch table was still out, three girls and two women seated around it. Cassie approached but didn't sit down, waiting for someone to speak to her.

One of the women looked up. She was smaller with short brown hair and a round, friendly face. She smiled at Cassie. "Hi, I'm Margaret. I'm your leader. You must be. . . ?" Her question trailed off in expectation.

Cassie put on a brave smile. "I'm Cassandra Jones."

One of the girls turned around. The one with short blond hair and a freckled face. Riley. "Oh, I know her," Riley said. "She's in my class."

"Well, great!" Margaret stood up and took Cassie's arm, guiding her to the table. "We're so excited to have you. And how nice that you and Riley are already friends!"

Riley hadn't spoken more than three words to Cassie since school started. But now she scooted over to make room. "You can sit by me." She pointed out the other girls. "That's Ciera, Leigh Ann, and Jaiden. There's Maureen. Her mom's our leader, but Trisha—" she pointed to the other woman, a taller woman with broad shoulders and wavy red hair. "She's the assistant leader. She's Jaiden's mom."

Trisha didn't smile at the mention of her name. She glanced up and stared at Cassie as if trying to figure out why she was there.

Cassie waited until Trisha looked down, then she whispered to Riley, "I don't think she likes me."

Riley shrugged. "She's moody."

Cassie nodded and shrugged it off as well. She tried to place all the names and faces together, keep them straight in her mind. "We're small."

"There'll be more," Margaret said, handing Cassandra a book.

Sure enough, more girls filed in. Cheyenne, Stacy, Kei, Janice. Still a small group, but not as bad as she'd feared. Her last troop had had about fifteen girls in it.

Margaret led them in a song and a game, and then they worked on their first merit badge: what to do in an emergency. They finished up with another game, then held hands and sang a song about friendship.

Riley didn't let go of Cassie's hand when they finished. She gave it a squeeze. "We're friends forever now."

"Yeah?" Cassie said, caught off guard but also hopeful. She could use another friend. She saw her mom's van pull up outside and gathered up her things. "Bye," she called, running toward the exit.

"Bye," the girls chorused back.

"See you tomorrow!" Riley said, waving.

Cassie let herself into the passenger side and plopped down with a sigh.

"How was it?" her mom asked, giving her a worried look.

"Great!" Cassie said, smiling. "It was great. I made lots of new friends."

CHAPTER FOUR

Blow Up

The week seemed to drag by. Cassie could hardly wait for Girls' Club again. Leigh Ann, Riley, and Maureen were in her class at school, and all three girls remained friendly with Cassie. Especially Riley.

Cassie and Danelle were heading for the swings at recess when Riley stepped over.

"We're playing freeze tag by the dome," she said. "Want to play with us?"

Freeze tag! Cassie loved the game. And she hadn't played it since they moved. "Sure! We'd love to." She looked at Danelle for confirmation, but Danelle wore a frown on her face.

"No, I don't think so," she said. "We like to swing."

"You could do both," Riley said, weaving her fingers together in front of her. "Play freeze tag and then swing."

Cassie watched Danelle's expression, but it didn't relent. "We'll swing first," Cassie told Riley. "Then we'll come join you."

"Sure," Riley said. She turned and walked away.

"You don't like freeze tag?" Cassie asked, trying to feel out why Danelle had reacted that way.

She grunted. "I don't like Riley."

"Really?" Cassie tried to think what Riley could have done to merit such a response. Sure, she hadn't said much to Cassie in the first week of school, but no one had. Riley was shy, just like Cassie was.

Danelle rolled her eyes. "She's so immature."

Cassie considered that statement as they swung higher and higher into the air. Riley was small for her age, but other than her size, Cassie hadn't noticed anything lacking in her behavior. "Did you guys used to be friends?"

"No, but we've known each other for forever. Trust me on this one."

Cassie couldn't stop thinking about Danelle's words all day. They never did join Riley's group for freeze tag, and Cassie felt bad about that. Only when school was out and Riley got up to head for the cafeteria did Cassie jump up and run after her.

"Riley!" she called.

Riley paused and waited, one eyebrow raised.

"Sorry we didn't join you at recess," Cassie said, catching her breath. "We decided to swing the whole time."

"Yeah," Riley said, nodding.

They walked side by side in silence before Cassie ventured, "So do you and Danelle know each other?"

"Not really. We were in the same preschool, but that was

like, forever ago."

Wow, Cassie thought. They'd lived around each other that long? Once again, she felt like the odd one out. But how could Danelle possibly know what Riley was like if they hadn't hung out since preschool?

They reached the cafeteria and joined the other girls around a table. Maureen's mom came over and talked to her a bit, then joined Trisha at the front.

"Today we're going to make stuffed animals," Trisha said, holding up a bear covered in plaid fabric. Next to her, Margaret smiled down at the girls, expressing all the enthusiasm that Trisha wasn't. "It's really very easy." She went on to demonstrate, and Cassie wished she could freeze-frame the instructions. She could tell already this would be confusing.

"So everyone, pick your fabric and I'll walk you through the instructions again."

Cassie leaned in with the rest of the girls, sifting through the pre-cut fabric shapes and choosing one she liked. "How is this going to be a stuffed animal?" she whispered to Ciera.

"Cassandra," Trisha said loudly, "I don't need anyone talking while I'm instructing. Please pay attention."

Cassie looked down, her cheeks warming under the chastisement. She tried to pay attention, but her ears buzzed with humiliation.

Everyone was working now, pulling a needle and thread along the edges of their fabric. Trisha was still explaining, but Cassie had missed the first directions. She turned to

Margaret, their leader. "I didn't quite get it. Can you show me?"

"Cassandra!" Trisha barked. "Around these parts, young lady, we show respect. If I'm talking, you're not. I don't know if you think you're something special or better than us, but if I have to tell you again to be quiet, you'll spend the rest of the time in your own special corner. Do you hear me?"

Cassie didn't even know how to respond. Her breath came in shaky little gasps, and she thought her eyes would pop out of her head. How could she talk to her that way? What right did she have?

"Answer me!"

All the girls were staring at Cassie, their faces reflecting the shock Cassie felt. She bobbed her head.

"Say, yes, Ma'am. That's how we talk in these parts."

"Yes, Ma'am," Cassie whispered. She fisted her hands together as tremors of anger swept through her. She bit her lip so hard she tasted blood. She wanted to call her mom. Now. She wanted to go home. She couldn't bear to be in the room with this ogre of a woman for one more minute.

Apparently satisfied that Cassie was subdued, Trisha went back to her instructions. Cassie put her piece of fabric down on the table. Without asking permission, she stood up and walked out of the cafeteria. She kept going until she got to the bathroom in the connecting hallway. Only once inside did she allow herself to release the tension she felt.

"How dare she!" she raged at her reflection. Her own wretched face stared back, tears rolling down her cheeks, her brown eyes bloodshot. "Who does she think she is? I was just asking for help! That witch!" She stuck her knuckle in her mouth and sobbed, but the anger was just getting going. She pulled her hand out and hit the mirror, screaming. "I hate her! I hate her! She's so mean, she's so awful! I hate this place, I hate her so much!"

A face appeared in the mirror behind Cassie. She met the eyes of Jaiden, Trisha's daughter. Jaiden turned around and went for the bathroom door.

"Wait, Jaiden!" Cassie cried out, panicking. She reached for Jaiden, anxious to draw her back, but Jaiden didn't wait. She went out, the door swooshing behind her.

Cassie gasped and wrapped her arms around her shoulders. She sobbed, rocking herself back and forth. She knew what Jaiden was doing. At this moment, she was tattling on Cassie, telling Trisha everything Cassie had said in the bathroom. If only she could flee. She should, she should run from here, leave the school. Never come back. She never wanted to talk to Trisha again. She couldn't stay in this group.

The door banged open, hard enough to hit the wall behind it. Cassie dropped her hands to her sides and braced herself. Trisha came in and faced her, lips pursed together and her arms folded.

"What's your problem?" she demanded.

All of Cassie's gusto left her. She tried to be brave. She did not want to cry in front of this woman. "Nothing," she whispered.

"I gave you very basic instructions. All you have to do is

follow them. And whatever you think of me, whatever your problem is, you have absolutely no right to come in here and badmouth me."

Cassie blinked, her eyelids feeling swollen and tight over her eyes. She couldn't reason with a madwoman.

"Now I expect an apology from you. Then you get yourself out of this bathroom and join us. With a good, respectful attitude."

"Sorry," Cassie murmured. She wasn't sorry, not in the least, but she was smart enough to know the only way she'd get out of this was by saying it.

Trisha grabbed the door and yanked it open. "Now go. And I better not hear you talking about this to anyone."

Cassie walked in front, clenching her teeth together.

CHAPTER FIVE
Recoop and Recovery

The girls were stitching up their bears, all of them looking more or less like Trisha's. Cassie shoved aside her piece of fabric and sat down at the table. She slumped over, putting her chin on her fist.

Margaret sat down across from her and picked up the fabric. "Can I help you with this?"

Cassie shrugged. She watched as Margaret put the bear together, but Cassie didn't offer to help. "Did she get you in trouble?" Margaret whispered.

Cassie's eyes burned again, and she closed them. She swallowed hard. *I just want to go home. This will all be over soon.*

A cool hand closed over hers, and Cassie opened her eyes to see Margaret staring at her, sympathy on her face. "I'm sorry."

Cassie nodded and looked away. A small part of her recognized that Margaret was an ally, but the bigger part of her felt betrayed. Margaret was the leader, not Trisha..

She could have stood up to her, defended Cassie. Even now she could tell Trisha she was in the wrong and Cassie hadn't done anything to deserve such treatment.

But Cassie understood that Margaret wouldn't do that.

Couldn't do that. She was too timid, and perhaps just as afraid of Trisha as Cassie was.

Cassie didn't speak to anyone the rest of the time at Girls' Club. Everyone finished up with their bears and started a game. Cassie fiddled with her bear, pretending to be too engaged in the project to play. She joined in the closing song only because Trisha called her out, and she'd rather stand there and lip sync than cause another scene.

Then it was finally over, and her mom's blue van pulled around to the side. Cassie grabbed her bag and dashed out.

"What's wrong?" her mom asked as soon as she opened the car door.

Cassie passed a hand over her eyes, knowing it must be obvious that she'd been bawling. Even now she felt the sting, the threat of more tears just below the surface. Her younger brother and sisters argued loudly in the backseat, and she let the noise invade her senses, dull the sharpness of the incident. She took a careful breath. "I don't want to be in this Girls' Club anymore."

Her mom raised both eyebrows. "Really? But you've been so excited all week."

Someone tapped on Cassie's window, and she turned to see Margaret there. Her mom pressed a button, and the window rolled down.

"Hi, Karen," Margaret said, giving a little wave. "I just wanted to talk to you about what happened today."

Cassie shrank back in her seat and avoided eye contact, wishing she didn't have to be here to overhear the conversation.

"What happened?" her mom asked, and Cassie detected a low note of warning in her voice.

Margaret hesitated, her eyes flitting to Cassie. "I didn't see all of it. But Trisha, the assistant leader, got on to Cassie rather harshly. Then Cassie went to the bathroom, and Trisha followed her. I'm not sure what happened then, but I think they had an altercation."

Her mom turned to her, danger flashing in her dark eyes. "She followed you to the bathroom?"

Cassie forced herself to nod. The prickling got to be too much, and the tears managed to work their way down her face.

Her mom turned her attention back to Margaret. "Thank you for telling me. It's Margaret, right?"

Margaret smiled. "Yes. Cassie's a great addition to our unit. My daughter Maureen really likes her."

"Thanks again. We'll talk later." Her mom rolled up the window, signaling the end of the conversation. She pulled the car away from the curb. "Cassie, what happened?"

"I don't really know," Cassie mumbled. "She just started yelling at me in front of everyone. So I went to the bathroom. Then she came in and yelled at me some more and made me come out."

Her mom kept her eyes on the road, but Cassie saw the way they narrowed. "That doesn't make sense, Cassie. Why would she just yell at you?"

Cassie exhaled. "She doesn't like me. I was talking to Margaret and she got mad about it. So I went to the bathroom to cry and yell and just vent, you know? But

Jaiden followed me in, and Jaiden told on me." She shrugged. "So that's what happened."

"And you don't want to go anymore?" her mom said in a softer tone.

Cassie shook her head. "No. I'm done with that group."

"Well, I won't make you go." She turned down the road that led out of the city and into the country. "We can look for another unit, maybe at a different school. But before we do, I want you to sleep on this and think really hard. It sounds like there are a lot of positives to this group. You have one leader who's really nice and likes you. You have friends. If you can deal with Trisha, you might be able to turn this negative experience around and still have a good time with these girls."

Cassie considered her mother's words. "I'll think about it." Right now, her feelings were so clear. She just wanted out of that group.

❦

Cassie didn't feel much better in the morning. She found a seat by herself on the bus and spent the ride drafting a note to Ms. Buckley, the school counselor. She wrote down everything that had happened. Fresh tears came to her eyes as she rewrote it, and her chin trembled with fury and indignation. No one had ever spoken that way to her before.

And truthfully, she regretted what she'd said, too. She'd been so angry, lashing out verbally and saying things she'd never say in person. Her shame made her feel black and dirty inside.

She finished her note before the bus arrived. She paused by Ms. Buckley's office and found the little mailbox for students to drop notes in. She shoved it inside and crossed her fingers. *Let Ms. Buckley find it soon*, she prayed.

She spent the rest of the day waiting. Her feelings were near the surface, and anytime anyone spoke to her, she found herself close to tears again. She kept glancing toward the door, hoping Ms. Buckley or one of her student helpers would appear.

At recess she told Danelle she wasn't feeling well. She didn't want to swing today. Instead she sat on the sidewalk and played with the grass, tearing up little pieces and searching for four leaf clovers.

Two shoes appeared next to her, and then Riley plunked down on the sidewalk. "Are you okay?" she asked.

Cassie nodded. She rested her chin on her knees and didn't meet Riley's eyes.

"Trisha's mean," Riley continued. "She always has been. I don't know why. Maybe she just doesn't know what to do around kids."

"Does she have any besides Jaiden?" Cassie asked.

"A little boy. He's like three or something."

"She shouldn't be a leader, then."

Riley shrugged. "No one else volunteered. Maureen's mom couldn't do it by herself."

Cassie supposed that was true, but she still didn't like it. "I'm going to switch groups."

"Really?" Riley fell silent. They both picked at the grass for a bit, adding the pieces they picked to a growing pile on the sidewalk. "Well, that's too bad."

Ms. Dawson blew her whistle. Students stopped their play and began to gather in from the corners of the yard.

"You should come over and spend the night," Riley said.

The invitation caught her off guard. She had a best friend, but so far Danelle hadn't invited her over. She'd expected that to be her first invite. But she quickly brushed it off. "That would be fun."

"Maybe this Friday?" Riley suggested.

"Okay," Cassie said. She felt a little bit of light crack through the blackness in her soul, breaking off a chunk of the dark. "I'll ask my mom."

❤

It wasn't until two days later that Ms. Buckley appeared in the classroom door. She waved at Ms. Dawson and then looked at Cassie.

"Cassandra," she said, beckoning to her.

Cassie put her pencils back in their box and shoved her work inside the desk. She stood up and followed Ms. Buckley down the hall, hands clasped in front of her.

They entered Ms. Buckley's office. As soon as the door was shut, Ms. Buckley turned to her, her short reddish-brown bob brushing the tops of her shoulders.

"I'm so sorry I didn't come for you sooner. I've been out of the office, and when I finally found your note, I realized how urgent it was. I could tell how distraught you were. How are you now?"

"I'm okay," Cassie said. "I'm doing a lot better, actually. It was really, really awful. But I'm okay."

"Would you like to talk about it?"

Cassie hesitated. "Well, I just don't know what to do about Trisha. I think she's an awful person. I was thinking about changing Girls' Club groups so I wouldn't have to see her anymore."

"Are you afraid of her?" Ms. Buckley asked, her eyes gentle.

"A little," Cassie admitted. "I don't want her to yell at me again. And I didn't even really do anything."

"So let's talk about how you can cope when someone overreacts. There's not much you can do to stop them. But you can control your feelings. How did you feel?"

"Angry," Cassie said. "I got too angry. I wanted to hurt something."

"That's normal, Cassandra. But you have to learn how to contain that. Or wait until the appropriate moment to vent it."

"Yeah," Cassie said. "I agree with that."

"Do you like Girls' Club?"

"Yes," she said without hesitation. "I love it. I've been doing it since I was five."

"Is Trisha so important to your life that you'd let her take away something you love?"

"No. But I can join a different unit and still be in Girls' Club."

"What about the friends you have here?"

Cassie thought of Riley. "I'll miss them."

"Is it worth it, Cassie? Or can you put Trisha into a small part of your mind as someone who's not important to you? And then shrug it off anytime she's mean to you?"

Cassie considered that. Could she? Was she strong enough to not let Trisha get under her skin? "I could try," she said slowly. "I guess I could give it another week, at least."

Ms. Buckley smiled at her. "I think you're a very brave girl." She turned around to her game shelf. "Now. Why don't we play a game before you go back?"

CHAPTER SIX

Sleepover

"Are you sure about this?" Mrs. Jones asked as she helped Cassie roll up the sleeping bag.

"Yes!" Cassie could hardly wait. Her first overnight since the move. She checked her duffel bag to make sure she had everything she needed. "Let's go! Riley said I could come over anytime after school."

"Patience!" Her mom laughed. "I already spoke to Mrs. Isabel. I know what time to take you. You need to make sure your chores are done first. Nobody wants to do them for you while you're off having fun."

Cassie uttered a groan but dropped her bag and headed for the kitchen. She unloaded the dishes as quickly as she could, stacking them into neat piles in the cupboards. The trash wasn't full, so she left it alone.

"Okay," she said, skipping into the laundry room where her mom sorted clothing. "I'm ready now!"

"I'm almost done with dinner," Mrs. Jones said. "Ask

your dad to take you."

"Dad!" Cassie raced toward the bedroom and plowed into her father as he came into the kitchen. "Mom said to tell you to take me to Riley's house."

He raised his eyes toward her mother. "Does Cassie know how to get there?"

"How would she know that? She's never been there." Mrs. Jones retreated to the dining room and came back with a sheet of paper. "Here's the directions."

He stuck them in his pocket. "Ready to go, kiddo?"

"Yes!" Cassie rocked back and forth on her heels with anticipation. Her first sleepover in Arkansas.

They piled into the car and headed back into town. The road changed from gravel to asphalt as they passed cookie-cutter houses and trailer parks. Her father finally turned into a large multi-plex apartment, similar to the one they had lived in before moving into their big house.

"Is this it?"

Cassie searched the parking lot for some identifying feature. One apartment had several potting plants overflowing on the ledge. "There!" She spotted Riley coming out the front door with two dogs in tow. "Yes, this is it!"

Her dad pulled up the rest of the way and parked in front of the apartment.

"Hi!" Cassie said, jumping out of the car.

"Hi," Riley greeted. She helped Cassie get her stuff inside. A tall man with long reddish hair stood in the kitchen. "Dad, this is Cassie," Riley said. "Her dad's outside."

"Well, I'll go meet him," he said, letting himself out.

"That's my dad, Len," Riley said, showing Cassie her room. It was down the hall and next to the bathroom.

"This is cool," Cassie said. "I like your house. It's cozy."

"The insulation's coming out." Riley kicked at a crack in the wall. "You can sleep on my bed, if you want. Instead of on the floor." She gestured to the sleeping bag.

"Sure!"

A little boy poked his head in and squirted Riley with a water gun. "Howard!" Riley screeched. She grabbed for him, but he'd already fled the house. She sighed and shook her head. "And that's my horrible little brother."

"Yeah." Cassie nodded. "I know that feeling."

"He knows your brother. Scott? I think they're in the same class."

"Oh, I'll ask him." Cassie glanced around the bedroom. She hadn't noticed another room in the house. "So where does Howard sleep?"

"At the end of the hall," Riley said. "With Mom and Dad. There's another room at the other end of the house, but it's a storage room right now."

"Ah." Cassie nodded her understanding.

"Cassie!" her dad called from the front room.

"Yeah?" she called back.

"Call me tomorrow and I'll come get you. Be good."

"I will!" she answered, rolling her eyes while Riley giggled.

"Are you hungry?" Riley led Cassie out of her bedroom

and back into the square kitchen.

Her stomach rumbled in answer. "Yes."

"You like ramen?" Riley opened a cupboard.

"Ramen?" Cassie echoed. "Like, Top Ramen?"

"I don't know." Riley held up a small crinkly package. "This is ramen."

"Yeah, Top Ramen! I love it!"

"Great. We just call it ramen around here." She tossed her the package. "Let's go eat it." She crossed the kitchen and opened the front door.

"Wait, like this?" Cassie followed her out to the parking lot, holding the package, perplexed. "Where are you going to cook it?"

Riley turned around, her green eyes sparkling. "You've never eaten it raw? Come on. You're going to love this."

Riley's dad was working underneath his big white pick-up truck. He had it parked on the grass next to the parking lot. Riley climbed up on the hood and helped Cassie join her.

"This is how we eat it," she said. She took the package from Cassie and opened it, then broke off a piece of the noodles. "Then you open the flavor pack." She ripped open the small foil packet. "And you just dip it in. See?" She stuck the noodles in the salty powder and pulled it out.

Cassie watched her bite into the powder-covered noodles. "All right, here goes," she said, tearing off her own piece and trying it. Her teeth crunched down on the raw ramen, and she nearly choked on the strong flavoring. Her eyes watered, and she laughed. "Yeah, it's good!" She preferred it cooked, but this wasn't bad.

"Yeah, I eat it this way all the time. Maybe every day."

The two dogs circled around the truck, barking and wagging their tails. Riley threw them a noodle, so so did Cassie.

"Yeah, I eat it this way all the time. Maybe every day."

The two dogs circled around the truck, barking and wagging their tails. Riley threw them a noodle, so so did Cassie.

"Don't feed the dogs," Riley said. "You'll spoil them."

"But you did," Cassie said.

"They're my dogs."

True. Cassie shrugged it off.

"So who's your best friend?" Riley asked.

"Danelle," Cassie said.

"Yeah? That's nice."

"Who's your best friend?" Cassie asked.

"I don't know. You, I guess."

"Me?" Cassie didn't know how she felt about that. Flattered, maybe, that someone else might like her that much. A little guilty, because she didn't consider Riley her best friend.

The dogs barked again, begging for Riley's attention.

"What are their names?" Cassie asked. They had one dog, Pioneer, named because he was the first animal in their new house, and one cat, a Siamese named Baby Blue. Cassie loved animals. She wished they could have a dozen more.

Riley pointed to the dogs. "That one's Itchy because he's always scratching, and that one's Shut it. No reason. And that one's Scaredy, because he always runs away from us. We can never get him to stay close unless we have him on a leash."

Scaredy. Cassie stared at him, the white and black mutt with a curvy tail and skinny little legs. "I want to hold him."

"He won't let you near him."

She had to try. Cassie hopped off the truck and held out her hand. "Here, boy. Come on, come here."

The dog put his ears down and tucked his tail in closer.

"Come on," Cassie begged. She whistled and clicked her tongue. "I won't hurt you."

He took several steps backward. Hoping to surprise him, Cassie dove at him. With a yelp of fear, the dog turned and ran for the open apartment door.

Riley sat on the truck laughing. "I told you."

Cassie climbed back up. "They're so cute! Can I keep one?"

She stopped laughing. "I don't think we can give them away."

"Let's ask your mom. I bet she says yes!" Cassie couldn't take her eyes off of Scaredy. She desperately wanted that dog.

"Tomorrow, Cassie," Riley replied. "She's not home right now, anyway. She's working tonight."

"Oh, okay."

Riley hopped off the truck. "Let's watch a movie."

♥

Riley's dad shut the dogs up in the laundry room for the night, where they howled and scratched and put up such a fuss that Cassie thought for sure someone would come knocking on the door.

But no one did. She must've fallen asleep watching the movie, because Cassie woke up once in the night to the staticky buzz of the television. She turned it off, used the bathroom, and curled back up on the living room floor next to Riley.

She woke up again when Riley's dad stepped into the house. "Good morning, Mr. Isabel," she said, as politely as she could.

"Morning," he replied in a gruff voice. He glanced at Riley still sleeping on the floor. "Want some breakfast?"

"Sure." Cassie sat down at the card table pushed up against the wall. A moment later, Riley's dad dumped two hot pieces of French toast on a plate and handed them to her with a bottle of syrup. "Thanks!"

Riley woke up and joined her, and Mr. Isabel made her some French toast also.

"Good morning, girls." A woman with similar facial features to Riley came out of the back room, running a brush through her short brown hair. Dark shadows ringed her eyes, and her voice was thick and groggy. "You must be Cassie. I've heard so much about you."

Cassie swallowed and said, "Hi, Mrs. Isabel. Thanks for letting me come over."

"Hi, Mom," Riley said. "Can we go for a walk today?"

"Yes, but stay on the sidewalk and don't go across the street. And don't go in any houses. And take the dogs with you."

A younger voice yelled from the back, "Can I go too?"

"And take Howard with you," Mrs. Isabel added.

Riley sighed. "Please, Mom? Just us?"

"No." Mrs. Isabel turned the brush on Riley's hair now, tugging her head as she combed. "I have things to do and need him occupied. Here, Cassie." She moved to the couch. "Come sit so I can brush your hair."

Cassie ran her fingers through her long brown hair, but didn't get very far before they got caught. She watched as Mrs. Isabel cleaned out the brush and put Riley's strawberry blond hair in a jewelery box already stuffed with hair. "Why are you keeping that?"

"For my dad," Riley answered from the table. "Someday when he goes bald, Mom's going to make him a wig."

"Really?" Cassie sat down in front of Mrs. Isabel. "Put my hair in, too!"

Howard stumbled down the hallway and came to stop in the middle of the kitchen. "I'm hungry," he announced.

"Well, eat fast," Riley said, clearing her plate from the table. "Or we'll leave without you."

They headed outside, but instead of walking through the parking lot to the sidewalk, Riley led Cassie behind the apartment complex and into the wooded ravine. The three dogs paraded behind them, tails wagging and tongues lolling. Cassie kept glancing back and whistling for Scaredy. Every time she did, he'd stop walking and duck down really low.

"Wait up, Riley!" Howard whined behind them, his legs pumping to reach them.

"Hurry, he's catching up!" Riley whispered. She grabbed Cassie's arm and hauled her down into the overgrown bushes.

"I'm coming, I'm coming," Cassie said, sliding down the leaves and hopping over branches.

He stayed close behind. They reached the bottom of the ravine, then turned around and started back up. Cassie spotted a large white house beside the apartment complex.

"Who's house is that?" she asked.

Riley looked up from the thorn bush she was gingerly extracting from her shirt. "Oh, that's the manager's house. Adrianne lives there."

"Who's Adrianne?"

"My mean neighbor. You're better off not meeting her."

"Mean neighbor?" Cassie widened her eyes. "What's so mean about her?"

"She steals your friends." Riley picked up a stick and broke it in half. "She tells people lies about you and acts all sugary and sweet."

"But your friends don't fall for it, do they?" Maybe they did. Maybe that's why Riley didn't have a best friend besides Cassie.

She didn't answer. She led Cassie to the sidewalk, and they started walking in the direction of Riley's apartment. The dogs and Howard were close on their heels. Cassie wanted so badly to hold Scaredy. He just wouldn't let her get close.

"Tick check!" Mrs. Isabel said when they came in.

This was new to Cassie. Riley stood still while her mom sifted through her hair and then checked her clothes. "Make sure you look yourself over when you change," Mrs. Isabel told her daughter. Then she turned on Cassie.

"What's tick check?" Cassie asked, following Riley's example while Mrs. Isabel lifted sections of her hair.

Mrs. Isabel chuckled. "That's right, you're not an Arkansan. Ticks are these little bugs that drop on you from the trees or crawl up from the grass. They latch on to your skin and stay there, sucking your blood. Anytime you go outside, you should check for them."

A shudder ran through Cassie, starting at her hips and going to her shoulders. "Sounds horrible!"

"Eh, they're not so bad. Normal. Just check for them."

Both she and Riley were tick-free. Riley plopped down on the couch and turned the TV on. Cassie joined her, though she'd never seen the show before and had no idea what was going on. Her parents were really strict about television. She only got to watch movies. Sometimes a TV show, but everyone had to agree on it, and with four kids, that wasn't likely.

The phone rang, and Mrs. Isabel answered it. "Hello, this is Rebecca. Oh, hi! Adrianne wants her hair braided? Sure, send her right over!"

Cassie glanced at Riley. "Is that the same Adrianne you warned me about?"

"Watch and see," Riley whispered. "She'll be so super nice to you."

She came to the door a few minutes later. Riley pulled Cassie outside.

"We don't need to watch her get her hair done," Riley said. "Boring, anyway."

"What's that?" Cassie pointed to the small yellow automobile in the parking lot. It hadn't been there when they got home from their walk.

"I don't know."

She and Riley approached it. Cassie stayed back in case it sprang to life and tried to run them over.

"Like my go-kart?"

They both turned around as Adrianne stepped down and joined them. She had wire-frame glasses, and her curly brown hair was held back in a neat French braid.

"That's how I got here," Adrianne continued. "I didn't walk. If that's what you thought." She walked right past Riley and gave Cassie a big smile. "Want to ride it?"

"Yeah, sure, can I?" Cassie said. "It looks fun!" And then she remembered Riley. Adrianne hadn't even said hello to her. "Wait, what about Riley?"

"Riley can ride this some other time. She lives here, right?" Adrianne rolled her eyes behind her glasses. "I'm Adrianne. What's your name?"

"Cassie. I'm Riley's best friend." The words popped out of her mouth unexpectedly, and Cassie couldn't take them back. Her face burned. She felt like a traitor.

CHAPTER SEVEN
Dog Fight

"Best friend?" Adrianne surveyed Riley again. "I guess you can both ride it. Cassie gets to go first."

Cassie climbed inside, her mind spinning. She nodded at Adrianne's instructions and then drove the little car in a small circle before returning it for Riley. While Riley rode around in it, Adrianne stood by Cassie.

"Do you like Riley's apartment?" she asked.

Cassie glanced behind her. "Sure." It had everything it needed.

"And all the dogs?" Adrianne arched an eyebrow.

Cassie pointed at Scaredy. "That one. I like him the most. But he runs away every time I try to touch him."

"I'll get him." Adrianne was off like a shot. Cassie couldn't help feeling some admiration at the way she crouched down and blocked the dog's every escape route. Finally, she caught him and returned with him in her arms, a triumphant smile on her face.

"What are you doing?" Riley was out of the go-kart, scowling as she approached them.

"She caught the dog for me!" Cassie held her arms out, breathless as Adrianne turned the trembling creature over to her. He shook in her arms, thin wiry tail wrapped around his little body.

"We can catch him ourselves, Cassie. Put him down."

Cassie ignored Riley's order. She sat down cross-legged in the grass, cooing at Scaredy and stroking his head. "Don't be scared of me," she whispered. "I love you."

Riley leaned against the garage wall. "Bye, Adrianne."

"Just trying be nice. Geez." She got back in her go-kart. "See you around, Cassie."

Cassie gave a little wave.

"See, she's evil," Riley said, shielding her eyes against the sun with one hand and glaring in the direction Adrianne had gone.

"Yeah," Cassie said, but with Scaredy in her lap, she could hardly condemn Adrianne. Finally, she was getting to hold the dog.

Riley turned to her with a big smile. "But you passed! She didn't steal you away from me! Best friends, right?"

Cassie hesitated. "Well, I'm still best friends with Danelle." She could have two best friends, she supposed.

Mrs. Isabel came out of the house, walking down the steps and coming outside. "You like that dog, Cassie?"

"I love him." Cassie's hands stroked his little shaking head, tried to calm his fast-beating heart.

"Do you want to keep him? I think we have enough dogs here."

Cassie lifted her head and uttered a gasp. "Really? Could I?" She wrapped her arms around him and cuddled him to her chest. Could he really be hers?

"Well, I've got to ask your mom."

"What?" Riley sputtered. "We're giving him away? Why? He's our dog!"

"The management said we could have one dog, honey," Mrs. Isabel said, reaching for Riley. "It's time for them to find new homes."

"Can we call my mom?" Cassie asked, unable to contain

her excitement.

"Sure. You'll have to put the dog down."

Reluctantly Cassie helped him out of her lap. She started to ask Riley to keep an eye on him, then thought better of it when she saw her face. Tears streaked down, her eyes swollen and red. She had her arms crossed over her chest and her lips pursed together. Cassie rubbed Scaredy's head. "I'll be right back."

This time, at least, she had her phone number memorized. She called home and crossed her fingers, hoping her mother would be agreeable. "Hi, Mom!" she said excitedly when Mrs. Jones picked up.

"Hi, Cassandra. How are you? Are you ready to come home? Your dad's about to leave to get you."

"No, not yet. But I have a question. The Isabels have a little dog they're trying to find a new home for. He's super sweet, really obedient, and so cute. Can I—"

"No," her mom interrupted before Cassie could even finish asking. "Don't even let that idea get into your head, Cassie. We already have Pioneer and Baby Blue. We're not bringing home any more animals."

"But, Mom, if you just saw him—"

"No, Cassie." Her mom's voice had taken on the stern, no-questions edge. "You can play with him every time you go to Riley's house."

Until some stranger takes him home. But Cassie kept the thought to herself. She knew better than to argue. "Okay," she sighed.

"Get your stuff together, Cassie. Daddy will be there

soon."

"Yes, Mom." She hung up the phone and turned around to Mrs. Isabel. "She said no," Cassie said, and she couldn't stop the disappointed tears that spilled over.

Mrs. Isabel wrapped her up in a hug, all softness and sweet-smelling. "It's okay. We'll have him for a bit longer still. Go outside and hold him while you can."

Cassie did as she was told, descending the steps and walking into the bright sunshine.

She spotted Riley right away, sitting on a wood crate and kicking her legs, staring into the distance.

"Hi," Cassandra said as she approached. She glanced around for Scaredy, but didn't spot him out in the open. "Where's Scaredy?"

Riley bobbed a shoulder in response.

Cassie felt a flash of annoyance. "Come on, Riley. You were out here with him. Where'd he go?"

"I put him away."

"You put him away?" Cassie rolled her eyes. "Okay, where is he?"

Riley pointed to a large draining culvert next to the sidewalk. "In the ditch."

Cassie stared at the ominous darkness in the giant pipe. She did not want to go in there. But how else would she get Scaredy back? She squatted at the edge and hesitated. She could make out shapes in there, but nothing for sure.

"I wouldn't go in there," Riley called. She hadn't moved from the crate. "There are snakes and rats."

Cassie swallowed hard. "Scaredy!" she called softly.

"Come here, boy!" She added a quiet whistle to the end. Nothing inside the culvert budged. She whirled on Riley, angry. "Why did you put him in there?"

"Because I don't want you to take him home," she replied, as if it were as simple as that.

"Well, for your information, I'm not taking him home! My mom said no! And now I don't even get to hold him until I go!"

Riley shrugged. "So? You're here to play with me, not my dog."

Was she actually jealous? Cassie couldn't believe it. "I'll just go call Adrianne and ask her to get him for me!"

"Go ahead," Riley shot back. "I'm sure she'd be happy to have a new best friend."

"*You* are not my best friend," Cassie breathed. "You're not even a friend."

Riley jumped off the crate. "Fine. Go get your stuff and don't come back to my house." She stormed off around the back of the house.

Cassie ran inside, stuffing her things in her bag and grabbing her sleeping bag.

"Everything okay?" Riley's mom asked from the kitchen sink.

Cassie took a deep breath. She wasn't going to complain to Mrs. Isabel about her daughter. "Yeah. I'm upset about the dog." Which was true. "My dad's on his way."

"We sure enjoyed having you, Cassie. I hope you'll come again."

Not likely. But Cassie only smiled and nodded. She had

her manners.

♥

Cassie spent the rest of Saturday fuming over the loss of the dog and Riley's behavior. She was angry at her mom, and barely spoke to her.

"Are they nice people?" she heard her mom ask her dad.

"Seems like it. Met both parents."

Cassie went to the room she shared with Emily. "Mom is so unfair," she said, tossing her overnight bag on the bed. "Riley's mom wanted to give me one of their dogs and Mom wouldn't let me have it."

"Really?" Emily looked up from where she rearranged her American dolls on the bottom bunk. "What kind of dog?"

Cassie lay down next to her and stared up at the top bunk. "I don't know. Small, white and brown. Maybe a beagle." She didn't have any idea, really, but at least she'd heard of that kind of dog.

"Maybe she'll change her mind. Did you have fun with Riley?"

She opened her mouth to say no, then thought better of it. "Yeah, kind of. She was mean about the dog. She didn't want me to have him." But they'd had a nice time, up until then. Cassie felt a prickling of guilt. She shouldn't have left Riley's house without saying goodbye, at least. She considered calling her, but didn't really know what to say.

♥

"Your dress needs to be ironed, Cassie."

Cassie's mom pulled an off-white, pleated dress out of

the closet.

"But I don't have time to iron it," Cassie said, taking the dress off the hanger. "Daddy said we have to leave for Church in ten minutes."

"Then wear a different dress." Her mom pressed her fingers to the bridge of her nose, a sign that she was fighting a headache. She was already dressed in a dark blue, floral print dress, her brown hair curled around her shoulders.

"How about this one?" Cassie pulled out a red one with a pinafore and white collar. Sundays were always so stressful, with her dad yelling and her mom trying to get everyone out the door in time. She didn't want to make it harder, but she didn't want to iron, either.

"That's fine. And brush your hair."

Cassie put the dress on and ran a brush through the tangles of her long hair. Then she stopped in front of her jewelry box. She loved jewelry, and she hated to let a day go by without picking out something sparkly to wear. She chose her favorite locket, a tiger eye on a thick chain. Then she picked out some clip-on pearl earrings and a pink wire bracelet.

She remembered before she'd gotten her ears pierced, her best friend Tammy bought her a whole sheet of stick-on earrings. Cassie had done her best to keep them sticky, putting them back on the sheet after using them. But inevitably, several would fall off when she wore them, and eventually she only had mismatched pairs.

It didn't matter now, because her ears were pierced, but she smiled at the thought of Tammy buying those for her.

Cassie knew she should write her a letter or call her, but every time she thought of it, she was in the middle of something. Like getting ready for church.

"In the car, everyone!" her dad yelled, and Cassie slipped on her black shoes and hurried out the door.

The church building looked much the same as the one they'd attended in Texas. Cassie wandered the halls until she got to the Sunday School classroom in the back. She followed a few other kids her age and closed the door behind her.

The teacher stood at the front, her wavy brown hair hitting her shoulders. "Hi, everyone, I'm your new teacher, Sister Garrett . Since I don't know you, I'm going to call roll." She picked up a piece of paper and cleared her throat. "Matthew Davis."

"Here."

"Gary Faucet."

"Here."

"Riley Isabel."

"Riley!" Cassie burst out. "I know her. She's in my class at school!"

"She's also in your Sunday School class," the teacher said.

"But I've never seen her," Cassie said. "She's never come here before."

"Well, then." The teacher smiled at Cassie. "Hopefully you can be the right kind of friend to bring her back."

Cassie frowned. She hadn't been that kind of friend when they were fighting.

Her teacher must've seen her hesitation, because she said,

"Just include her, Cassie. Invite her to hang out with you and your friends. Join your activities."

She could do that. Maybe Riley would enjoy hanging out with her and Danelle. Their fight was stupid, after all. She made up her mind to apologize the next time she saw her. Maybe they would all be best friends.

Episode 2: Club Girls

CHAPTER EIGHT
Ice Cream Treat

Monday.

Cassie ignored the butterflies in her stomach as she entered her fifth-grade classroom. The weekend had been rather emotional. For the first time since moving to Arkansas, she'd spent the night at a friend's house. But because of the stupid fight over a dog, Cassie wasn't sure if they were still friends.

She waited in the bathroom during break and cornered Riley as soon as she came out of the stall.

Riley hesitated, something like fear flashing across her face before her green eyes hardened. "What do you want?" She lifted her chin, the short strawberry-blond hair just grazing her neck.

"I wanted to apologize," Cassie said. "I was rude to you at your house on Saturday. And I had a nice time before that." Before Riley hid the dog from Cassie, anyway. "I want to be friends again."

Riley hesitated, and then the stiffness left her shoulders. "Why?"

"Well. . . ." Cassie hadn't really expected that question, and she blurted out the truth. "Because they called your name at church, and we're supposed to be friends!" She followed Riley to the sink and squirted soap on her hands.

"They said my name at your church?" Riley squinted at her over the water, both of them washing their hands. "But I don't go to church."

"I know." Cassie nodded. A few strands of her straight brown hair had escaped her pony tail, and they floated around her face. She slicked them back. "But you're supposed to. This is why we're—" Cassie hesitated to use the term, but she did. She crossed her fingers that Danelle, her first friend in Arkansas, wouldn't hear. "Best friends."

Riley lowered her eyes, but not before Cassie saw her smile. She smiled too, glad that they weren't fighting anymore.

Cassandra had just moved to Arkansas from Texas this year, and the first few weeks of school had been confusing, both mentally and emotionally, as she tried to figure out her role and make new friends. She considered herself lucky now; she had two best friends, Danelle Pierce and Riley Isabel. The two girls didn't like each other, but Cassie figured as long as she kept them apart, that didn't matter.

"I'll ask my mom about why they mentioned me at your church," Riley said as they exited the bathroom and got back in line in the hallway. "She'll know."

The class continued down the hall for P.E. Cassie partnered up with Danelle for catch.

"What's going on with you and Riley?" Danelle asked, the metal from her braces reflecting the overhead lights in the cafeteria. "You're like, all buddies now."

Cassie didn't know if she should feel guilty about having two best friends, but she did. "I spent the night at her house on Friday. We're really good friends now."

"You've never come to my house," Danelle said, tossing her the ball.

Danelle had never invited. "I'd love to come. Or you come to my house," she said instead. She tossed the ball back.

"I saw you reading *The Babysitters Club*. Do you like those books?"

"Love them!" Cassie said, brightening. She loved to read more than anything else in the world. "Do you like them?"

"Yeah, I've read a few of them. They're fun."

"We should start our own club!" Cassie gasped, catching the ball again. She and her sister Emily had already talked about doing that, but just the two of them could hardly make up a club. "You, me, Riley—"

"Riley?" Danelle interrupted, wrinkling her nose.

Cassie didn't want to leave Riley out. "Well, three people isn't very many."

Danelle hesitated. "I guess we could try it. I don't know, though. She's so annoying."

Cassie was too excited about Danelle agreeing to worry

about her jibe toward Riley. "I can't wait! It's going to be so much fun!" She envisioned them sitting around her room with the telephone, waiting for people to call them and schedule babysitting assignments, just like they did in the books. She tossed the ball again to Danelle, who laughed.

"I'll tell my mom. Call me and we'll plan when to come over."

♥

Cassie waited until Ms. Dawson had finished giving them a workbook assignment and the class was too occupied to notice her. Everyone had their books open, pencils scribbling, when she stealthily removed her reading book from her desk. She opened it up just to be sure. All twenty squares had a sticker in them, proof that she had read twenty new books since the beginning of the school year. The reward was an ice-cream trip with her fifth-grade teacher.

She pushed back her chair and tiptoed to the desk, the book tucked under her arm. "Here," she whispered, dropping it in front of Ms. Dawson. She started back to her seat when Ms. Dawson said, "Come here, Cassie."

Cassie turned around as Ms. Dawson opened the book. She raised one eyebrow. "You've already read this many books?"

Cassie nodded. "I love to read."

Ms. Dawson looked at her, one eye squinting slightly. "Can you make a list of all the books you read?"

"Um, sure." She hoped she could remember them, anyway. She sat down, her heart pounding with the added pressure. She knew she should start on her workbook assignment, but she needed to write down these book titles before she forgot!

It took some thought, but most of the titles came easily enough. She'd read several from the same series, and that wasn't too hard to remember. But she got to number eighteen and couldn't think of the last three books. She took the sheet back to Ms. Dawson, blinking hard so she wouldn't cry.

"I can't remember the last three. I'll have to go home and look through my books."

Her teacher tilted her head and read through the list. "That's all right, Cassie. This is good enough." She looked up and smiled. "I'll call your mom today and set up a time to take you out for ice-cream."

Cassie beamed back at her. "Okay!" She skipped back to her chair and finally got started on the assignment.

♥

"So your teacher called me today," Mrs. Jones said as Cassie unloaded the dishwasher. "She said she wants to take you out for ice-cream."

"Oh, yeah!" Cassie turned around. "It's okay, right? It's because I already read twenty books."

"Of course it's fine. I think it's great that your teacher is so involved."

"Yeah, she's awesome." Cassie turned back to the dishes, thinking of something else. "Can we start a babysitters club?"

"A what?"

"I'll show you." She put the last cup in the cupboard, then ran out of the room to get one of her books. In the back was a flier that said, "Start your own babysitters club!" It listed the steps needed to get something like that going, followed by testimonials from other girls who had successfully started their own clubs.

Her mom took it from her hand and read over it. "Do I need to pay for anything?"

Cassie shook her head. "No. We'll spread the word and meet here once a week, and people will call us to babysit."

"Well, I guess that's okay. Who do you want in your club? Are you including your sister?"

"Yes."

"Sure. You can start it."

Cassie squealed and threw her arms around her mom's neck. "Thanks so much!"

♥

Cassie gathered Danelle and Riley at recess the next day.

"I got permission to start the babysitters club," she said, squeezing their fingers excitedly. "My mom said you can come over on Thursday night and we can get started. Does that sound good?"

"Yeah," Danelle said, nodding. "I'm in."

"I'll ask my mom," Riley said. "But I think I can do it.

Cassie looked at her two friends, Riley with short strawberry-blond hair, Danelle with shoulder-length brown hair and braces. She had so much hope that they'd become great friends, also.

♥

"You can sit up here with me." Ms. Dawson opened the passenger door to her long, silver car and gestured for Cassie to get in.

Cassie did, though she felt very awkward climbing into her teacher's car. She folded her hands together in her lap and sat up straight.

Ms. Dawson started the car. "I'm very impressed that you read all those books so quickly. You must really like to read."

Cassie nodded. She relaxed a little bit in her seat. "Yeah. It's my favorite thing to do."

"Have you ever tried writing?"

"Writing?" She'd never really thought about it. It sounded so boring. But then she remembered the two stories she'd started in fourth grade. "I started some silly stories last year, but I haven't really written since then." Silly stories, all right. One about an evil monster who became friendly, and another about four orphans who had to move in with their aunt. Neither story got past the third chapter.

"It's been my observation that people who like to read also like to write."

Cassie didn't like writing down notes in class, and she hated copying things off the blackboard. *I might be the one reader who proves that wrong*, she thought.

They pulled up to the ice-cream shop, and she followed Ms. Dawson inside.

"What would you like?" Ms. Dawson asked.

It just seemed wrong to tell her teacher to buy something

for her. Cassie surveyed the menu behind the counter. "Could I have a vanilla waffle cone, please?"

She sat down at a booth and waited while Ms. Dawson placed the order. What would they talk about? Tomorrow's assignment? Her grades? This just seemed so weird.

"So," Ms. Dawson said, returning with the ice cream, "what do you think of Arkansas so far?"

If she had asked Cassie a few weeks ago, the answer would've been very different. "I like it, I think. It's different than Texas. But I'm making friends. I like the school." And now that they were moved into their new house, everything felt better. "We have a dog and a cat. I want another dog, but my mom won't let me have one."

"One dog can be enough."

Cassie shrugged. "Yeah." Riley had a dog that Cassie just loved, and Riley's family was willing to give it to the Joneses. But Cassie's mom put her foot down on the idea.

They chatted about Cassie's family and the new house, and then Cassie's ice-cream was gone. They got back in the car and Ms. Dawson turned to Cassie.

"Where do you live, Cassandra?"

Cassie squinted at the road, not even sure where she was. She tried to visualize the turns her mom made when she picked her up from school once a week. Not that it did much good, because they weren't even at the school. "Go left," she said, because she was pretty sure left was the correct direction.

Ms. Dawson pulled out onto the main road. Seven minutes went by before she ventured, "Am I supposed to turn anywhere, Cassie?"

There were farther out of the city now, with empty pastures and fields dotting the road beside out-buildings and antique shops. "I'm not sure," Cassie admitted. "This looks familiar. We turn left somewhere in here, but I'm not sure where."

Ms. Dawson gave her a look that Cassie couldn't identify. Exasperation? Frustration? Annoyance? She sank into her seat, willing herself invisible. Great. She'd just managed to ruin things with her teacher.

Ms. Dawson pulled the car over into a gas station. She fished around in her purse until she found a cell phone. "I'll call your mom and get directions."

Cassie nodded but didn't say a word. She figured the less she talked, the less Ms. Dawson would remember being upset with her.

"Hi, Karen, this is Ms. Dawson, Cassandra's teacher. Yes, I'm fine, how are you? Listen, we have a small problem here. No, no, nothing urgent." She laughed. "I'm bringing her home, and she can't remember how to get there."

Cassie squeezed her eyes shut, her face burning with humiliation.

"We're at a gas station right off the highway. Oh, okay. Uh-huh. Sure, I got it. We'll see you soon." She put the phone away and slid the car out of the gas station. "It's all right, Cassandra. We're on the right road, we just didn't go far enough."

Cassie uttered a sigh of relief. At least she hadn't led them miles off course or into a different city.

Ms. Dawson made a left turn at the next signal, and everything began to look more familiar. The curvy, two-lane road, the trees hovering over the tops of it, the cows and ponds.

"Oh, this looks right," Cassie said.

"Yes, your mom thought you'd start to recognize it as we got closer." She slowed down on some of the tighter curves. They came around a corner, and Cassie pointed to the statue of a big white bull standing guard at the top of a gate.

"That's the white bull." It was what her mom always told her to look for because it meant she was going the right way.

Ms. Dawson didn't comment. Several minutes later, she made the final turn up the gravel road that led to Cassie's house. She slowed down around the potholes, the car churning and fuming as it climbed the steep hill. "No one could expect you to remember how to get here, Cassie."

She'd never called her by her nickname before. Her teacher wasn't mad at her. She didn't think Cassie was ridiculous for not knowing the way home. Cassie's shoulders relaxed.

Ms. Dawson pulled into the circle drive in front of Cassie's home. Their new house. They'd only moved in a few weekends ago.

"This is a lovely home, Cassandra," Ms. Dawson said, getting out of the car.

"Thank you." She grabbed her backpack and slid out also. She spotted her mother coming down the porch steps.

"And thanks for the ice-cream."

"It's a pleasure to have you in my class, Cassie."

Her chest warmed under the praise. She nodded and hurried into the house, leaving her mother to talk to Ms. Dawson.

CHAPTER NINE
Smart Kids

"Are you doing Odyssey of the Mind?" Emmett Schrimmer asked Cassie during math. He and Matthew Grace sat closest to her.

"I don't know what that is," Cassie replied, penciling in her answer on her paper. It didn't look right, so she erased it and tried again.

"It's this really hard contest for smart kids. You have to build things and answer creative questions."

Matthew rolled his eyes. "It's not for smart kids. It's for anyone who's interested."

"Yeah, but only the smart kids are interested," Emmett returned.

"Why are you asking?" Cassie asked, interrupting their argument.

"Well, we form teams," Emmett said. "And we need one more person on our team. You could do it." He lowered his voice. "The coolest part is, we get to leave class twice a week to practice."

That was a very appealing thought. "Okay. I'll do it."

"Great!" Emmett said. "My mom's the coach. I'll tell her you joined."

The next day Cassie took home paperwork for her mom to sign. "I need you to sign this," she said. "Or I can't join the Odyssey of the Mind team."

"What's that?" her mom asked.

"A team for smart kids. And we get to leave class to practice."

Mrs. Jones frowned. "I've never heard of it. I'll take a look at this."

Cassie hovered close by, waiting for the coveted signature.

"Don't you have chores to do, young lady?" her mother said, shooing her off. Cassie sighed and went to unload the dishwasher.

She finished, and her mom still hadn't supplied her with the paperwork. Cassie went back to her mom's room. "Well? Did you sign it?"

Mrs. Jones put down the book she was reading and straightened her glasses. "It's a lot of practices and a huge time commitment. Not just in school, Cassandra, but after school too. And if you commit, I commit. Are you sure you're going to do it?"

Cassie nodded, quite certain this was what she wanted. "Yeah. It'll be fun."

"All right." Her mom sighed like it physically hurt her, but she signed her name on the dotted line. "Here you go."

♥

Cassie joined Emmett and a handful of other kids as they were let out of class after lunch. "So what do we do at practice?"

"Well, first we have to see if you like it."

"If I like it?" Cassie frowned. "What's there not to like?"

"Maybe you won't think it's fun? I don't know. And you have to feel comfortable with your teammates. You'll be working on challenges with them."

"I thought I was on your team."

"Well, kind of." He raised his eyebrows at her. "It depends on where you're needed, also. We always have a challenge practice, and we're scored on our participation."

"What challenges?" Cassie could feel the beginnings of panic building in her chest. No one had said anything about performing in front of anyone. "Will I be doing that today?"

"Yeah. Don't worry. We all do it. It's easy."

She was definitely panicking now. Cassie's breathing came in fast and hard, and she curled and uncurled her fingers, trying to get life back into them. "I changed my mind. I don't want do to this."

They came to a stop outside another classroom door, this one set up very differently than the others. It had four tables inside and one podium in front.

"You'll be fine," Emmett said again. He slipped past her into the room.

Cassie wanted to turn and run back to class. Instead she came in with the rest of the students. She hoped no one could see the way her knees wobbled.

"Hi, I'm Mrs. Holland," a woman standing by the door said. "I'm the teacher in charge of special events here at Walker. You must be Cassandra Jones?" She consulted a piece of paper in front of her, one with Cassie's mom's signature spread across the bottom. "We're excited to have you. Sit at a table, please."

Cassie nodded and turned around. The other students had all sat down, four to a table. That left only one with a spot. The one at the very end. Cassie recognized Janice from Girls' Club and sat by her.

"Hi, Cassie," Janice said, scooting her chair over to make room.

"Wait, she's on our team?" a boy that Cassie didn't recognize said.

"These aren't your official teams," Mrs. Holland said, standing at the podium at the front. "We'll organize teams later. Right now we're just going to run through some drills. This is the trivia part. Team A, you'll start. You can discuss the answer as a team, but only the team captain answers. Decide quickly who your team captain is going to be."

The other kids all seemed to know each other, so Cassie stayed quiet as her team (Team D) argued and decided on Jerry Freeman, the boy she didn't know, as the captain.

"Question one. What food makes up nearly all of a Giant Panda's diet?"

Team A leaned toward each other and deliberated back and forth before Emmett stood up. "The bamboo."

"That is correct." Mrs. Holland made a tally mark on the board. "Team B. True or false? Mice live for up to ten years."

Were all of these questions about animals? Cassie could only hope she'd get a true or false one. She straightened up as it neared her team's turn, her heart hammering so hard in her chest she thought she'd throw up.

"Team D. What is the name of the phobia that involves an abnormal fear of spiders?"

Her team huddled up. "It's a phobia," Jerry whispered. "So it probably has the word phobia in it."

Janice nodded. "Like claustrophobia."

"So something phobia," the other boy, Kayne, said. "What's another word for spider?"

"Insect?" Jerry suggested.

Janice shook her head. "Spiders aren't insects. They have eight legs, not six."

"Time's almost up," Mrs. Holland said.

Cassie held very still, hoping no one would remember her if she didn't move.

"If they're not insects, they're arachnids," Kayne said.

"Arachnid phobia?" Janice said.

Jerry snapped his fingers. He stood up and said, "Arachnophobia."

"That's correct." Mrs. Holland gave their team a tally mark.

"How did you know that?" Janice asked.

"I saw a movie once with that name, all about crazy spiders." He grinned, obviously pleased with himself.

They fell silent as the other teams went through their questions. Cassie tried to guess the answers before the team captains shouted them out, but she didn't know them. Not any of them.

"Team D," Mrs. Holland said, turning to them again. "What is the largest type of big cat in the world?"

Big cat. Cassie listed them in her head. Tiger, cheetah, panther, lion, cougar. But she couldn't begin to guess which was the largest.

"Lions are huge," Jerry was saying. "They can weigh like five hundred pounds."

"So is that our answer?" Janice asked.

"Are we sure they're the biggest?" Kayne asked.

Jerry turned to Cassie. "Don't you have any guesses?"

There it was, the direct question. Cassie's face burned. "I don't know. Maybe a panther?"

Jerry rolled his eyes. "A panther isn't a type of cat. It's another word for big cats like leopards and jaguars."

"Oh." She shrugged. "The jaguar, then."

"Time!" Mrs. Holland said.

Jerry stood up and faced the front. "The lion."

Mrs. Holland shook her head. "Sorry, that's incorrect. The correct answer is, the tiger."

Jerry glared at them all as he sat down. "Thanks a lot."

"None of us knew, Jerry," Janice said, pushing her short brown hair behind her ear.

"Yeah, well, some of us know nothing at all." His gaze fell on Cassie.

She turned away, humiliation warming her neck and face. She didn't want to do this anymore. At least her mom would be relieved not to have to drive her to all the practices.

"This next part is a problem for all of you to work out as a team. Take ten minutes," Mrs. Holland said, going to the board. She wrote several sentences and then stepped to the side.

Cassie squinted at the board, but Mrs. Holland's handwriting was slanted and tiny. She couldn't make out the words.

"What species should we use?" Janice asked.

"Something with a small name," Jerry said. "Like cat or dog."

"But that's too easy," Kayne said. "It would be more creative to do a longer name. Like chinchilla or guinea pig."

"I like chinchilla," Jerry snorted. "The chinchilla eats a quesadilla."

Janice laughed, her shoulders shaking. "You so don't pronounce the l's in quesadilla."

"So? It rhymes." He looked at Cassie. "You just don't have any opinions about anything, do you?"

"I don't know what we're doing," Cassie admitted.

"Wow, shockers," Jerry said. "You can't read, either? What are you even doing here?" He looked around the room toward Emmett's table. "I'm gonna have to talk to Emmett about who he invites here."

Cassie blinked, close to tears by his harsh words. "I can't see the board."

"Right," he snorted.

Janice shot him a glare and swiveled in her chair to face Cassie. "We're making rhymes with animals. We decide which animal and make a rhyme, like, 'the cat is wearing the hat.' Got it?"

Cassie nodded, but she wasn't really listening. She didn't care anymore. She stood up. "I have to use the bathroom." She walked over to Mrs. Holland, ignoring the way Jerry and Kayne leaned together and started whispering. "Mrs. Holland? Can I go to the bathroom?"

"Sure," Mrs. Holland said. "We only have about five minutes left. You can just go back to class when you're done."

Cassie exhaled in relief. "Okay."

"How were things today? Did you get the hang of it?"

Cassie faked a huge smile. "Sure. It was fun."

"Perfect. Will we see you next week?"

"Um, I don't know," Cassie said, shifting her weight from one foot to the other. "My mom said it might be hard to work into her schedule."

"But it's during the school day."

"I know. I mean, all the other practices. I'll let Emmett know." Cassie gave a brief wave and fled the room before Mrs. Holland could ask any more questions.

She bypassed the bathroom entirely. She didn't really need to go. She just had to get out of that room that made her feel *claustrophobic*, away from those arrogant people who made spiders seem friendly.

CHAPTER TEN
Glasses

"Today we'll have an eye screening," Ms. Dawson said on Friday. She finished writing their spelling words on the board. "After you've written your sentences, line up at the door."

Eye screenings were nothing new. Cassie remembered doing them every year at her old school. "Look at the apple," they always said. But she never needed glasses.

She glanced around at her classmates, noting those who had glasses and those who didn't. Glasses were like one more piece of jewelry. And they made people look smarter. Both of her parents had glasses, so it was just a matter of time before she needed them too. Or so she hoped.

The kids trooped down the hall to another room where several computers were set up. Cassie waited in line patiently until it was her turn.

"What's your name?" the parent volunteer asked.

"Cassandra Jones."

The woman wrote that down on her sheet of paper, other

students' names cascading down in a row. "Ms. Dawson's class?"

"Yes."

"Okay." She put the pen down and repositioned the machine, lowering it down to Cassie's height. "Put your chin right here and press your forehead into the top bar."

Cassie did as instructed.

"Can you see the red apple on the picnic table?"

She saw it with perfect clarity. "Yes."

"How about now?"

She squinted, but it was still clear. "Yes."

"Okay." The image changed to rows of letters. "Can you read me the letters on the second line?"

"E A F G P." The last letter was B, but Cassie pretended like she couldn't see it.

"And the third line?"

These were blurry, but Cassie could read them. G B C D E. "O P C D B."

"And the fourth line."

A F E B G. "I can't read them."

"All right, thank you, Cassandra."

Cassie dutifully backed away from the machine, letting someone else take her place. She squeezed her fingers together. It probably wouldn't mean anything. She probably hadn't done bad enough to need glasses. She pushed the thought from her head and decided not to wonder about it for now.

Easier said than done. Cassie kept thinking about the screening over the next few days, wondering when she'd know, if she'd know.

She didn't have to wait too long. A few days later, the intercom buzzed.

"Ms. Dawson?"

Ms. Dawson stopped in the middle of her lecture. "Yes?"

"Can you send Ciera Lamb, Emmett Schrimmer, Maureen Hemming, and Cassandra Jones to room two-thirteen, please?"

"Yes, Ma'am." Ms. Dawson nodded at the four students.

Cassie jumped up and joined them, eager to get out of the classroom and find out why they were needed. She knew the two girls well from Girls' Club, and Emmett had continued to be friendly even after she dropped out of Odyssey of the Mind. "What do you think it is?" she asked as they walked through the halls. She thought of the eye screening. It was all she had thought about for days.

"I don't know," Emmett said.

"Maybe we failed our eye exam," Cassie said, pressing the issue.

"I hope not!" Maureen said, her blue eyes going wide. "I don't want glasses!"

"I would love them." Cassie's hand dropped to the beaded necklace she wore, fingering the large plastic baubles. "I think it would be so fun."

Sure enough, they walked into the classroom and saw the same machines set up as last time. Cassie's heart rate sped up. Should she lie again? She couldn't even remember what she'd said on the first one. What if she got it wrong?

It went much faster this time. Their names were already

on a list, and a man called them out one by one. When it was Cassie's turn, she sat at the machine as instructed. He skipped the apple part and went straight to the lines.

"Can you read the first line?" he asked.

That one was easy. "Yes," Cassie said, and recited the letters.

"The second line?"

She could. She licked her lips. She opted for just mixing up the letters.

"And the third line?"

She shook her head. "It's blurry." Which was true, but she could still see everything.

"All right, thank you, Cassandra. You can go back to class."

She was the last one, but her classmates had waited for her.

"You were right," Ciera said. "It was about the eye exams."

"I sure hope I passed this time," Maureen said.

Cassie was pretty sure she hadn't passed.

♥

"Cassie." Ms. Dawson came to her desk right before school ended and handed her a slip of paper. "Put this in your backpack and give it to your mom, please."

It was folded in half so Cassie couldn't see the words, but she was dying open it. "Okay." She'd take it out on the bus and read it.

She sat down by Betsy Lemo. Betsy was in a different class, but since they rode the same bus, they were friends.

"What's that?" Betsy asked as Cassie retrieved the piece of paper from her backpack.

"A note from my teacher."

"Oo, you in trouble?"

"Of course not," Cassie scoffed. She unfolded the note.

"And you're going to read it?" Betsy gasped. She leaned in closer.

Cassie pulled it away, holding it above her head. "You can't read it! I have to know what it says before I give it to my mom."

Betsy rolled her eyes. "That's kind of like cheating."

Cassie ignored her and read over the note.

Mrs. Jones,

Cassandra failed her second eye screening this morning. Please make an appointment with the optometrist of your choice to verify if she needs to use corrective lenses.

"Yes!" Cassie exclaimed, pumping her fists in the air.

"What, it's something good?" Betsy said.

"I need glasses." Cassie couldn't stop grinning.

"And that's good news?"

"Yeah!" Cassie shook her head. "I've been wanting them for years! I'm so excited!"

Her mom wasn't quite as excited. She made an appointment for the following day, and as they drove to the doctor, she said, "Glasses are expensive, Cassie. You can't change your mind or quit wearing them just because you don't want to anymore."

"I'll love them!" Cassie exclaimed, offended her mother

would even think she might not.

Her mom grumbled under her breath and didn't say anything more.

The doctor was quite thorough, asking Cassie all kinds of questions before even pulling up the letter chart. He made her a bit nervous. Somehow she felt he'd know if she lied about what she could see.

Finally he sat her down in the chair and had her recite the letter lines.

Cassie squinted a little bit and took her time, pausing on some letters as if they were hard to make out.

"Thank you, Cassie," he said when she finished. He jotted down a few notes and turned to her mother. "So it does look as though she has a little bit of myopia. She could probably get by without glasses, but these things tend to get worse with age. If you don't do it now, you'll be doing it next year."

Cassie held her breath while her mother considered. Finally Mrs. Jones turned to her.

"What do you think, Cassie? Should we do glasses now or wait?"

"Now!" Cassie burst out. She hopped from the chair. "Can I go pick out my frames?"

Mrs. Jones gave a helpless shrug. "I guess so."

The doctor followed them out of the examining room. "These are the kids' frames," he said, leading them over to a wall with smaller, colorful frames.

"These are nice," her mom said, picking up a pair of burgundy wire ones.

Ew. No way. Cassie wrinkled her nose. She spotted a pair of thick, turquoise frames and pulled them loose. She let out a gasp. They had sparkles and colored dots mixed inside the plastic, extending all the way through the arm that hooked over the ear.

"These, Mom! I love these!"

"Those?" Her mom arched an eyebrow.

"Oh, those are quite popular with the kids," the receptionist said with a chuckle. "All the bright colors."

"Yep." Cassie held them out. "Can I wear them home?"

"Oh, no, honey." The receptionist came around her desk and stood with Cassie and her mom. "Now that you've picked out your frames, we'll order them from the company. They'll put in your lenses so that when the glasses come, they're made for your eyes and your eyes only."

Cassie frowned. She'd envisioned walking out of here with her new glasses on, and showing up at school tomorrow all decked out. "How long's that going to take?"

"Oh, about two weeks." She looked down at Cassie through her own wire frames and smiled. "Not long. They'll be here before you know it."

Cassie nodded and put them back, trying to hide her disappointment. Two more weeks. Two whole weeks before anyone even knew she'd gotten glasses.

CHAPTER ELEVEN
Club Meeting

Thursday evening finally arrived. Cassie and Emily took the family phone into their room.

"I hope the battery doesn't die while we're using it," Cassie commented, hands on her hips. She surveyed everything they'd set up for their first Babysitters Club meeting. "People are probably going to be calling all evening."

"You girls have everything you need?" her mom asked, poking her head in the room.

"Yep," Cassie and Emily chorused.

Cassie ticked the items off on her fingers. "We've got the phone. The appointment book. A pencil, of course. It's almost time!"

As if on cue, the doorbell rang. Emily bolted from the room, and Cassie ran after her.

"Hello!" a man's voice boomed from the doorway.

"Hey, Steve!" Mr. Jones said enthusiastically, grabbing his arm and pumping it. "So you're Danelle's father!" He looked at Cassie. "I work with him, Cassie."

"Wow," Cassie said. "That's cool." She grabbed Danelle's arm and hauled her into her room.

Danelle giggled. "Your dad's funny."

"Yeah," Cassie agreed.

Danelle took off her sweater and sat down on the bed. She looked around Cassie and Emily's room. "I like your decorations."

Cassie glanced around, too, wondering what Danelle liked. There was a poster of Dalmatians on the wall and a collection of American Girl dolls on the bed frame. But that was it. Maybe she liked the wallpaper? "Thanks." Emily nudged her, and she added, "This is my sister, Emily."

"Hi," Danelle said. "I've seen you around. Is Riley coming?"

"Um. . . ." Cassie checked her watch. Just a little after seven. "She said she was." She stared at the phone. "I could call her, I guess, but what if someone tries to call while I am?"

"You just click over to the other call," Danelle said. "You know how to do that, right?"

Actually, no. Cassie hardly ever used the phone. "Oh, right. I can do that." She grabbed her address book from under the bed, glad she'd written in Riley's phone number. She dialed the number.

"Hello?" Mrs. Isabel's voice answered.

"Hi, this is Cassie. Is Riley there?"

"Hi, Cassie. Sure, hang on one moment."

A second later, Riley got on. "Hello?" she said, not

sounding very enthusiastic.

"Hey, we've started our club meeting. Aren't you coming?"

Silence followed on the other end. Finally Riley said, "I can't tonight."

There was no further explanation. Cassie rested her head against the wall. What could she say? She could guilt-trip her and make her feel bad for ditching. Or she could try to make her convince her parents. Neither would work, though. Riley wasn't coming. "Okay, well, we'll miss you," she said instead, and hung up. "She's not coming," she announced.

Danelle raised her eyebrows and settled back on the bottom bunk. "Well, I guess that's not a big surprise, is it?"

Cassie wondered again what the deal was between Danelle and Riley. "Let's get started, then! I'm calling this meeting to order." She sat cross-legged on the floor, facing the other two girls. Opening one of her notebooks, she said, "Date. October 3. Members present: Emily Jones, Cassandra Jones, and Danelle Pierce." She tapped the pencil eraser against her lips. "Anything else I should write?"

"That we're awesome!" Danelle said, making a fist and thrusting it in the air.

Cassie put the minute book down and opened her appointment book. "Now we just wait for people to call."

The three of them stared at the phone. Cassie willed it to ring.

"We could play Uno while we wait," Emily said.

The phone began to jingle. Cassie had never thought of it

that way before, but it wasn't really a ring. It was a melody. She dove for it, but Emily was faster.

"Did you need the Jones' residence or the Babysitters club?" she asked.

Cassie groaned. Claudia had her own phone line in the book, which meant no one had to guess if the caller wanted her or her family.

"Oh, you want to talk to him?" Emily's face fell. "Sure, I'll get him." She pulled the phone away and whispered, "It's for Daddy."

Cassie grabbed the phone and took it down the hall to the living room. "Daddy. Phone's for you." She handed it to him, but didn't let go. "Hurry! We're having our meeting right now!"

"I'll be quick," he said, locking eyes with her and nodding solemnly.

Emily had the Uno game out when Cassie returned and was dealing out cards. Cassie couldn't think about the game. She sat on her hands, tapping the carpet with her toe. Someone could be trying to call right now. Would her dad click over? He knew how to do that, right?

Someone tapped on the door, and then her dad poked his arm in, phone extended in his hand. "Any luck yet?" he asked.

"Not yet," Cassie said, taking the phone. "Did anyone call while you were on it?"

"Nope. No one."

No one else called during the entire hour. They finished up their game of Uno, and then Danelle's dad was back to get her.

"I'm sure it was because it was our first night," Cassie said, trying to keep her spirits up. "Next Thursday will go better."

"I"m sure that's all it was," Mr. Pierce said. "Night, Jim."

"Night, Steve!" Mr. Jones said, all big smiles.

Cassie rolled her eyes and went back to her room. What a bummer of a night.

♥

"How was your club meeting last night?" her mom asked her when she got off the bus Friday. "You went to bed so fast, I didn't get the chance to talk to you."

Cassie unloaded her backpack on the kitchen table. "It didn't go well," she said, zipping it shut. "Nobody called."

"Well, it was your first meeting," Mrs. Jones said. "I'm sure it will go better."

These were the same things Cassie had told herself the night before, but today she wasn't in the mood to be placated. "And what if it doesn't?" She crossed her arms over her chest and faced her mom. "If people don't call us to babysit, our club is pretty worthless."

"Didn't you have fun anyway?"

She considered the question and lifted one shoulder. "I guess." But that wasn't the point. It wasn't supposed to be a fun Uno club.

"I've got a babysitting job for you," Mrs. Jones said.

"You don't count," Cassie said in frustration. "I always babysit for you. You don't pay enough, anyway."

Her mom burst out laughing. "Well, let's think about

this." She pulled out a chair and sat at the table. "Come, sit."

Cassie heaved a sigh and sat.

"What did you do to prepare for your babysitters club?"

"Well, I invited babysitters. We took notes, role, and waited. As soon as we get our first appointment, I want to make fun babysitting bags to take with us. I have some ideas for that."

Mrs. Jones nodded. "These are all great things, Cassie. How did you get the word out about your club?"

"Get the word out?" Cassie echoed.

"Yes. Who knew about your club? Who did you give your phone number to so they could call and hire you?"

"No one," Cassie said, feeling her heart sink like an anchor. Why hadn't she thought of that? No one would call her if they didn't even know.

"Well, that at least is something you can change," her mom said. "Let's make up some fliers tonight for your club, and tomorrow you can take them through the neighborhood and hand them out to everyone."

Cassie nodded, the anchor lifting from her heart and her spirit lightening. "Okay! That's a good plan."

Cassie's mom helped her design a simple black and white flier on the computer. They didn't have a copy machine, so Cassie counted up the houses in the neighborhood to see how many she needed to print.

"There's the Davidsons, the Maguires—but they only have a dog—"

"Take them one anyway," her mom said. "They might

know someone with kids. Or maybe they have nieces and nephews."

Cassie nodded. "The Coys, the Webbs, the Thompsons, the Howards, the Rodriguezes, the Ruperts, the Lorries, and. . . ." That was it. Their rural community only had a small spattering of houses. And most of those didn't have small kids. "There's a few houses on the other street."

Her mom shook her head. "You're not allowed to walk down there. Give some fliers to Danelle and Riley, and tell them to hand them out to their neighbors."

Cassie thought of Riley's apartment complex and nodded, but she knew Danelle's neighbors were just as spread out as hers. "I'll take some to church, too."

"Good idea. Print off about forty, then. Ten for each of you and ten for church."

Forty sounded like a great number. She started the print job and waited for the pages to come out.

♥

Cassie woke up to the sounds of her younger brother and sister running through the house, laughing and yelling. She wasn't ready to get up yet. She didn't want to. She rolled over and squeezed her eyes shut, pretending like she hadn't woken. The bed felt so delicious and comfortable, and Saturday was the only day she got to sleep in.

Her eyes snapped open as she remembered the fliers she and her mom had made. Today was a special day. This was the day she would get her club going!

"Good morning. Glad to see you up before nine," her dad said when she came in for breakfast. He had his grubby clothes on, and Cassie tensed. She needed to hurry and lay out her plans for the day, or he'd have her out in the garden, picking up rocks.

"Good morning. I'm delivering fliers through the neighborhood to advertise my babysitting club," she said in a rush, pouring a bowl of cereal. She stuffed a spoonful in her mouth to keep from saying anything else.

"Oh. How very entrepreneurial of you."

Cassie squinted at him. She'd heard that word before, but she couldn't think of what it meant. "Which is?"

"Very businesslike. Very professional." He finished making himself a shake and left the room.

Cassie mapped out her plan. She'd start at the bottom of the hill and work her way back up. If she started at the top, by the time she finished she wouldn't want to climb back up.

She combed her hair nicely and put on a headband to keep it out of her face. Then she added a gold chain with a medallion of a young girl and her favorite earrings, a pair of lime-green springs.

"Mom!" she called. "I'm going to hand out my fliers!"

"All right!" her mom called back from downstairs.

Cassie gripped the fliers in her hands and went outside. The crisp autumn air greeted her, but she knew by the time she reached the bottom of the hill, it would be warm. It was almost a full mile from her house to the end of the street.

Sure enough, when she reached the bottom twenty minutes later, she was not cold at all. She walked up to the Rupert's house and knocked on the door.

"Well, hello, Cassie!" Mrs. Rupert said, answering. "What are you doing down here?"

"My friends and I have started a babysitters club," Cassie said, reciting her rehearsed speech. "Here's a flier that tells you all about it. We'd love to babysit your children anytime you need us. Just call that number on the flier on Thursday evenings." She paused here in case Mrs. Rupert wanted to say something.

"Thank you, Cassie, what a lovely idea," Mrs. Rupert said.

"Thank you!" Cassie replied. She turned and trotted down the driveway, quite pleased with how that had gone.

Cassie continued her way up the hill. A lot of people weren't home, so she stuck fliers in their mailboxes. Everyone was very polite, smiling and thanking her, and Cassie felt optimistic that they'd start to get some business.

The last house was the Maguires. They were the ones that didn't have kids, but her mom thought she should go there anyway. Cassie started down their long, blacktop driveway, clutching her remaining fliers and humming to herself.

The driveway led into a four-door garage, while the house sat to the left of the driveway. Cassie turned toward the house when a low growling stopped her. She swiveled in the direction of the sound to see a large brown dog approaching her. He had his head low between his shoulders.

Another growl to her right made her gasp. She jumped around to see a second dog there. Her heart battered at her throat like a bird in a cage, seeking a way out. *Don't act afraid*. She'd heard that somewhere before, right? "Hello, doggies," she said. "Nice doggies." She held out a hand, noting how it shook.

The dog snarled and lunged at her, and she took a step backward. *Help*, she thought. She wanted to turn around and run, but she knew, just knew, that these dogs would chase her up the hill. She met one of the dog's eyes, trying to give it the impression that she couldn't be intimidated.

She thought she'd seen the Maguires pull into the driveway right before she got here. Maybe they would hear her. "Mr. Maguire!" she shouted.

Immediately both dogs launched into a chorus of barking and snarling. One skittered backwards on his feet, he was so wound up. The other dove at her, snapping and barking.

Cassie screamed. She couldn't help it; she was officially terrified. The dog stopped a few feet from her, but both of them continued the threatening barking. Cassie gave up on any semblance of calmness and screamed as loud as she could.

CHAPTER TWELVE
New Dog

Cassie stared at the dogs, trying to keep both in her line of sight. They stared back at her, saliva dripping from their snarling mouths. What would her mom do when she didn't come back? Would the dogs tire of her before she got tired of standing here staring at them? Would someone come looking for her?

Her only hope was to attract the attention of whoever was inside. She screamed again, so loud her throat ached. Her ears rang, but the dogs barked harder, and she doubted anyone heard her. She put her hands over her ears, too frightened even to cry.

The front door opened, and Mr. Maguire stepped out. He was an older gentleman with a bald spot on the top of his head. He wore suspenders over a striped shirt. "What's all this ruckus, fellas?" he began, and then he spotted Cassie.

"Down, boys," he yelled, clapping his hands. "Back away!"

Obediently the dogs stopped. The stubby little tails dropped, and the dogs skulked back to the garage.

"What are you doing here?" Mr. Maguire said. "Are you hurt?"

Cassie shook her head, though her whole body trembled. "I was screaming."

He looked at her, his gray eyes apologetic. "I didn't hear you, hon. I came out to see why the dogs wouldn't stop barking. You shouldn't wander over to people's houses that you don't know."

Cassie couldn't agree more. She held out a flier, waited for him to take it. Then she walked back up his long driveway, hoping her shaky legs wouldn't give out on her.

♥

"I can't believe you were attacked by dogs," Danelle said, taking the fliers Cassie handed her at recess.

"Not attacked," Cassie corrected. "Just threatened." She looked at Riley and hesitated. "Do you want some?"

Riley shrugged. "I don't know if I'll be able to come."

"Well, take some anyway." Cassie put a few in her hands. "Hand them out to your neighbors. Maybe they need babysitters too."

"Yeah, okay."

"This is great." Danelle tucked her fliers into her back pocket. "I'm sure we'll have more callers next time."

"Why couldn't you come last time, Riley?" Cassie ventured. She didn't want to cause an argument, but she felt like they deserved to know.

"No one wanted to drive me."

That made sense. Riley didn't have any control over that. "Well, maybe someone can drive you next time."

"Maybe."

❤

Cassie spooned some rice onto her plate and waited for the grilled chicken to make its way to her. "I gave Riley and Danelle fliers. I'm pretty sure we'll have plenty of people calling on Thursday."

"That's great, honey." Her mom met her dad's eyes across the table and smiled at him.

Cassie glanced at her dad, not sure if her parents were flirting with each other or laughing at her.

"Are you doing okay after those dogs attacked you?" Mr. Jones asked, accepting the bowl of rice from Emily.

Cassie scowled. "They didn't attack me. I was frightened, yeah, but I wasn't hurt."

"I just mean, will you be okay around other dogs?"

"Of course," she scoffed. "I'm not suddenly thinking every dog I see is going to hold me hostage in someone's driveway."

"I'd be scared," Annette said. "I'd never go near a dog again."

"You're afraid of everything," Scott said.

"No, just mean things," Annette protested.

"She's only four," Cassie said, shooting a glare at Scott. "She's allowed to be scared. Leave her alone."

The doorbell rang, and Scott and Annette pushed away from the table, already racing for the door.

"Who would come over now?" Cassie said, glancing at her mom. To her surprise, her mom's eyes were crinkled in a smile.

"Why don't you go see?" she replied.

Curious now, Cassie got up from the table.

"Hi, kids," a familiar voice was saying from the entryway. "Is your mom here?"

Cassie rounded the corner and saw Mrs. Isabel standing there. Riley stood behind her, holding Scaredy in her arms. Cassie cocked her head and frowned.

"Oh, hey," Riley said, spotting her. She gave a smile, but it trembled around the edges. "Here." She held out the dog.

"Hi, Karen," Mrs. Isabel said, her eyes looking over Cassie's shoulder. "I hope we're not late."

"Right on time," Mrs. Jones said, placing a hand on Cassie's arm. "Cassie, aren't you going to get your dog?"

Cassie whirled around, her eyes going wide. "My dog?" she gasped.

"Unless you're afraid, of course," her mom teased.

Cassie faced Riley, unable to believe it.

"Here," Riley said again, shoving Scaredy into her arms.

Cassie let out a shriek of joy, and the dog cowered, his whole body trembling. His tail curled around his leg, and a pebble of poo hit the carpet. Cassie didn't care. She held him against her. "Mine? He's mine." She pressed her face to his and rubbed his nose.

"Yours," her mom confirmed.

Scott started up a chorus about how he wanted a dog, and Emily joined in, but Cassie paid them no mind. She thought of Riley and looked at her friend anxiously, worried she would be angry.

But she was smiling. "He'll be happy here. And I can come see him."

"Absolutely!" Cassie exclaimed. She reached over and hugged Riley, her throat suddenly thick. "Thank you, thank you, thank you. Thank you so much."

♥

Cassie didn't know the first thing to do with a dog. It didn't take more than an hour to figure out that it was potty training. She took the dog for a walk, but he didn't poop. They came back in the house, and he found a cozy corner of the living room to relieve himself. The next hour she tried again, and still nothing. And the next hour.

"How often do I have to do this?" she asked her dad.

"Every hour," he replied. "It's the only way the dog will learn."

She got ready for bed and brought Scaredy into her room, where he crawled under her bed and trembled.

"He can't sleep with you," Mrs. Jones said, coming into the room. "We need to bathe him first and get him house broken. Tonight he'll sleep in the bathroom."

"In the bathroom!" Cassie gasped out. "He'll hate it there!"

"He'll get over it," her mom promised.

She and her mom laid down newspapers on the bathroom floor and gave him a bowl of water. Their other dog, Pioneer, kept poking his head inside to see what was going on. At least he was a friendly dog and didn't seem threatened by Scaredy.

Cassie hated closing the door on him, leaving him there, but she did. She lay in bed thinking about him, so glad he was hers and wondering how he was.

And then the whimpering started. It was so quiet, Cassie wasn't sure she'd really heard it. She held very still and strained her ears. There it came again. A quiet, mournful sound. It didn't get any louder, and she doubted anyone else could hear it. Cassie snuck out of bed and tiptoed to the bathroom. Pressing her ear against the door, she listened. Sure enough, the faint cry came from inside.

She opened the door and went in, turning on the light so she could see. Scaredy cowered by the toilet. The newspapers by the bathtub were peed on, but the rest of the bathroom was clean. Cassie got a towel from under the sink and put it on the floor. Then she turned off the light and lay down on top of it.

♥

Cassie woke up sometime during the night. She had no idea what time it was; the bathroom was pitch black. Her legs felt cold, but not her chest. Curled up beside her, little body lifting and lowering with each breath, was Scaredy. A happy feeling settled in her throat and filled her body. Cassie wrapped her arm around him and went back to sleep.

Or tried to. A moment later the bathroom door opened and shoved into her back.

"Ow," Cassie said.

The light turned on. Scaredy stood up and scurried

behind the toilet. Emily stared down at her. "What are you doing in here?"

"Keeping the dog company." As if that weren't obvious. "He was crying."

"Well, the alarm went off. Better get ready for school."

"Did you wake Scott?"

"Not yet." Emily pulled the door closed, and Cassie assumed she'd gone to wake their brother.

She went behind the toilet and clicked her tongue, brushing her thumb and forefinger together, beckoning to Scaredy. He took two tiny steps toward her, and Cassie petted his little head.

"You'll be safe here," she told him. "And as soon as I get home, I'll come and see you."

The day dragged on at school. Riley asked how Scaredy was, but she lost interest about two minutes into Cassie's enthusiastic explanation about how last night had gone and what he was doing now. Cassie told Danelle instead, who thought it was cool that she had a new dog.

"What kind is he?" she asked.

"A beagle," Cassie replied, though she had no idea if that was true. It didn't matter to her. But she got the feeling it would matter to Danelle.

"Cool," she said. "Can't wait to see him on Thursday."

In Girls' Club after school, they started a cross-stitching project. It was fun, and Cassie enjoyed picking out the pattern and then choosing her thread. But her mind kept going back to the little dog waiting for her at home. When she saw her mom's blue van, she pushed her project back in the box and shouted a goodbye as she ran out the door.

"How is he?" she asked, shutting the car door and turning to her mother.

"Ask Annette," her mom replied. "She's been playing with him all day."

A stab of envy pierced Cassie's heart. She knew she should feel grateful; she should thank Annette, and be glad that Scaredy wasn't home alone and sad all day. But really, she was jealous. Would the dog like Annette more now? She gave her little sister a weak smile. "Thanks for doing that. How is he?"

"Great!" Annette said cheerfully, kicking her legs in her booster chair.

As soon as Mrs. Jones parked the blue van in the driveway, Cassie hopped out of the car. She ran into the house and made a bee-line for the hall bathroom. Scaredy lifted his head from his front paws and blinked at her when she came in. He didn't run and hide, and Cassie's heart warmed.

"Hello," she cooed, setting her backpack on the sink. "How are you?" She got out her homework assignment and sat down on the toilet with it. Today she'd get her work done in here, with her dog.

CHAPTER THIRTEEN
Multiplication

"Today we're going to do a multiplication test," Ms. Dawson said, setting a timer on her desk. "For those of you who haven't done this before, I'll hand out the test face down. You leave it that way until I say go. It has one hundred problems on it, and you'll have one minute. When the minute is up, mark the spot you got to and then finish up the test."

Cassie sat up straighter, clasping her hands together on her desk. She shoved thoughts of Scaredy from her head and focused on the task at hand. Her last school had put a huge emphasis on the times tables. She'd memorized almost all of the single digit multiplication, and was quite certain she could finish this test in one minute.

Ms. Dawson placed a test face-down on her desk, and Cassie put her finger on the edge of it, pencil ready. Her heart did a drum roll in anticipation.

"All right," Ms. Dawson said, returning to her desk. She

picked up the little white timer and spun the dial. "Ready, set, go."

Cassie flipped her paper over and started writing down the answers. Each problem drew the answer from her brain as if it were a magnet. For the past three years her teachers had drilled these in, putting a huge focus on sight recognition. It was paying off now. Forty-nine, eighty-one, sixteen. Her pencil couldn't move as fast as her brain did.

She was almost there. She didn't dare look at the timer as she started on the last row of problems. Sixty-four, nine—

"Time!" Ms. Dawson called. "Everyone put a line on your paper so I know how far you got. And then do the rest."

Cassie exhaled as her heart rate slowly descended, disappointment replacing her excitement. She drew a line after problem number ninety-four. She still had six more. She finished them up, turned her paper over, and put her pencil on top. She glanced around at her classmates, still working hard on their problems. No one else had finished.

"Are you done?" Emmett whispered beside her.

"I think so," Cassie said, not wanting to sound too confident lest he think she was boasting.

"Already?" Sara Berry said. Cassie could see from where her pencil hovered that Sara had two more rows to go.

Cassie nodded. She reached into her desk and pulled out *The Babysitters Club* book she was reading.

"Anyone still working?" Ms. Dawson asked. When nobody raised their hand, she smiled and walked to the front of the room with her answer key in hand. "All right, let's check. Whoever didn't miss any will get a prize."

Cassie looked at the six she hadn't finished in time. She knew she wouldn't get a prize.

Ms. Dawson began calling out the answers. Cassie felt a sense of pride as she checked off each one. So far she hadn't missed any.

"Yes!" Brenna Atkins whispered loudly.

Nobody paid her any mind. Brenna often drew attention to herself during class.

Ms. Dawson called out the next answer.

"Yay!" Brenna squealed.

The teacher called out another.

"Yes!" Brenna said, not even whispering. She pumped her fist.

Cassie tried not to roll her eyes. Apparently they were going to get a to-the-second update on Brenna's score.

Ms. Dawson kept going, and Brenna kept cheering for herself all the way to the end. Cassie did her best to tune her out. In spite of not finishing on time, she was quite pleased that she hadn't missed any.

"Did anyone get a perfect score?" Ms. Dawson asked.

"Me! Me!" Brenna's hand shot up so fast and wiggled so hard that it lifted her from her chair.

Cassie frowned, her stomach giving a little jolt of displeasure. She knew Brenna hadn't finished before the timer went off. She'd watched her finish up her test long after Cassie had turned hers over. But she kept her mouth shut. It was none of her business if Brenna wanted to cheat and lie. She swallowed hard.

"Let's see, then." Ms. Dawson took Brenna's paper and

started going over it. "Oops, nope, Brenna, you missed one." She circled a problem with her red pencil and handed it back. "Sorry."

Brenna heaved a sigh and sank back in her chair.

"Anyone else not miss any?" Ms. Dawson's eyes surveyed the room.

"How many did you miss, Cassie?" Sara asked.

Emmett peered over his desk at Cassie's paper. "You didn't miss any. Raise your hand."

"I finished after the timer went off," Cassie said.

"You didn't miss any!" Sara hissed, grabbing Cassie's paper.

"But I didn't finish!" Cassie protested, trying to retrieve her test from Sara.

"Ms. Dawson, Cassie didn't miss any," Sara said loudly, holding up the paper.

"I didn't finish before the timer went off," Cassie said, hating that she had to rat herself out.

"That doesn't matter," Ms. Dawson said, approaching their desks. "Did you miss any?"

Cassie shook her head.

Ms. Dawson took the paper and stood there as she went over it. Then she handed it back. "Congratulations, Cassandra. You didn't miss any." She returned to the front and faced the class. "Not only did she not miss any, but Cassie only had six left when the timer went off. Bravo, Cassandra. You did fantastic."

Cassie's face warmed under the praise, but her heart swelled with pride. Her classmates congratulated her.

Cassie murmured her thanks, keeping her eyes lowered. But inside she glowed, pleased that she excelled at something, at least.

CHAPTER FOURTEEN
End of a Club

Cassie ran home from the bus stop and headed straight for the bathroom. Her mom stopped her.

"You don't have time to play with the dog right now. We have somewhere to go."

Cassie paused with her hand on the doorknob. "Where are we going?"

"To the eye doctor." A smile quirked around the edges of her mother's mouth. "Your glasses are here."

Cassie let out a squeal of delight. "Let me just say hi to him real quick."

Twenty minutes later they arrived at the doctor's office in downtown Fayetteville. Cassie jumped around from foot to foot while her mother spoke to the receptionist.

"We're here to pick up some glasses. Cassandra Jones."

"Oh, of course." The woman smile and disappeared into a room in the back. She returned with a white case and pair of bright turquoise glasses in her hands. "This look familiar?"

Cassie squinted at them. It had been so long, she couldn't be sure.

"Let's look in the mirror." She directed Cassie to the mirror next to the kids' glasses and placed them on Cassie's face. "How do those look?"

Everything sharpened to the point of being slightly too close. She tilted her head. The large round frames made her eyes seem smaller behind the lenses. She pulled them off and examined them. Sure enough, they had the colored, floating polka dots inside the plastic. She put them back on and smiled at her reflection. She looked different.

"What do you think, Mom?" she asked, meeting her mom's eyes in the mirror.

"They look great, Cassie. They're the ones you picked out, right?"

"Right." Cassie nodded, examining herself again. She gave a nod. "Yeah. I like them." It would take some getting used to, though, especially when her vision changed at the corners of her eyes.

♥

She almost forgot to put her glasses on in the mad rush to get to the bus the next morning, but at the last minute remembered. She slid them on, a bit apprehensive. What would her classmates think? She trapped her long dark hair behind a headband and gave her reflection a cursory glance. She looked tired, but she'd spent the night in the bathroom again, so that wasn't too surprising.

She climbed on the bus and looked for Betsy, who got on before her. She spotted her hanging over the back of her seat, poking Chad Cameron with her pencil. Cassie plopped down next to her, and Betsy turned around.

"Hey!" she exclaimed. "You got glasses!"

"Yep." Cassie beamed, excited that she'd noticed right away.

"How fun! Do you like them?"

"Love them," she said, sliding her backpack around to her chest. "Do you?"

"They look great! Everyone's going to love them."

Cassie straightened up in her seat, feeling more confident already.

♥

"I love your glasses," Danelle said at recess. She and Riley and Cassie sat under one of the trees, picking dandelions and looking for four-leaf clovers.

"Thanks," Cassie said. "You're coming over tonight, right?"

"Yep. My dad's bringing me."

"And you?" Cassie looked at Riley.

"Yeah," she said, "I think so."

"Did you guys hand out your fliers?"

"I did," Danelle said. "My mom took them to work and handed them out, also."

Riley didn't answer, and Cassie didn't press her. That meant she hadn't.

Ms. Dawson blew her whistle, and the three girls stood up.

"I'll see you tonight!" Cassie said.

♥

Danelle was the first to arrive, at about five to seven. Outside, the night air had turned nippy, so Cassie took her jacket and hung it up. Mr. Pierce went into the living room to talk to Mr. Jones.

"Riley's not here yet," Cassie said. "Come see my new dog."

Scaredy had graduated from the bathroom and moved to her room. She'd walked him outside earlier and considered him successfully house trained. He lifted his head from Cassie's blanket and batted his little tail against the ground, a soft *thump thump thump.*

"Oh, he's cute!" Danelle said, crouching down in front of him. He backed his head up but didn't stand.

"Yeah, he used to be so scared of us." Cassie sat next to him and patted his head. "I think he likes us now." As if on cue, he got up and crawled into her lap.

Emily came in with a bag of chips and a plate of cut fruit. "Snacks! It's seven."

"Great." Cassie opened up the notebook and took attendance. "Riley's not here," she stated.

"And she's probably not coming," Danelle added.

Probably. Cassie decided not to comment on that. "Well, it's time! Let's see who calls today!"

They waited wordlessly for the first five minutes. Cassie got up and got everyone water during the five after that. Emily offered to braid Danelle's hair, which annoyed Cassie, but Danelle said yes, so there wasn't anything she could do about it.

A knock sounded on the door, and then Mr. Jones poked

his head in. "Anyone call yet?"

"Not yet," Cassie said, mustering a smile. "But I'm sure they will soon!"

"I'm sure," he replied. He closed the door.

The silence that followed felt heavy with expectation. Cassie studied her nails to avoid making eye contact with anyone else.

"What happens if no one calls?" Emily ventured.

Cassie didn't answer. She didn't know what to say.

"Someone will call eventually," Danelle said.

"But how long do we wait?" Emily pressed. "Do we keep meeting every Thursday, hoping that someone calls?"

Cassie bristled, annoyed with her little sister. "First off, Emily, you're only here because Mom said I had to include you. You're nine years old. No one's going to hire you to babysit."

Emily's brown eyes filled with tears. "Well, you're only ten!" she sputtered, and ran from the room.

"But I'm almost eleven!" Cassie shouted after her.

"Ten is a bit young," Danelle said. "I won't be eleven until next summer. Maybe we should try again in a year."

Cassie hunched her shoulders, feeling her grand idea deflating like a balloon with a hole in it. She knew in her gut that if they didn't make it work this time, they wouldn't try again. "I've been babysitting since I was nine."

Danelle shrugged. "Sure, but nobody else knows that."

Her eyes stung and she sniffled, trying to hold back the emotions. One tear snuck over the side, and she wiped it away. "So we should quit?"

"Maybe just for now," Danelle said. Her eyebrows lifted in a gesture of sympathy. "But we can try again when we're older."

"Yeah. Okay." Cassie put on a stiff smile. She knew this was the end. She tried to think of something more to say, something that might make Danelle want to come back every Thursday, but words failed her.

Danelle stood up. "Well, I guess I'll get my jacket. Thanks for trying this, anyway. It was fun."

Cassie folded her arms and nodded, not believing for one second that Danelle had enjoyed these meetings. Boring and unproductive. Cassie felt like a total failure.

Mr. Jones came and put his arm around her shoulders as Danelle and her dad left. "So that's the end of it?"

A tear rolled down her cheek and she sniffed. "I guess."

He gave her a squeeze. "It was a good effort, Cassie. I'm excited for what you'll do in your future."

Not Cassie. She didn't even want to think about tomorrow.

"Cheer up, sweetheart." He nuzzled her hair and winked at her. "Your mom and I have a surprise for you guys."

"Really?" Her curiosity piqued, managing to dull some of her disappointment. Who didn't love a good surprise? "What is it?"

"We'll tell you at dinner tomorrow. Now come on. Let's go on out."

Episode 3: Road Trip

CHAPTER FIFTEEN

Family Vacation

"We have an announcement to make," Mr. Jones said as the family sat down to the traditional spaghetti Sunday dinner.

Cassie perked up. The announcement. Her dad had mentioned last night that he had a surprise, and she'd been anxiously waiting since then. She glanced at her mom. Was she finally pregnant? She'd been trying for so many years, everyone had kind of given up on the idea. "What is it?"

"Hold your horses," her mom said, extending her hands out to the children on either side of her. "After prayer."

Cassie obediently took her mother's hand in her own and her sister's hand with the other. Once everyone's hands were held, her father bowed his head and said a blessing on the food.

"Amen," Cassie echoed, then lifted her head to study her mother. "Well, what is it?" She ignored the bowl of spaghetti that came her way.

"We're taking a family vacation later this month."

"But we have school," Emily said. "How can we go on a vacation?"

"Well, we'll have to pull you out of school. That will be okay, right?"

"Yes!" Scott cheered. Just six years old, he hated everything school related.

"Vacation, that's cool," Cassie said, finally piling some noodles on her plate. Hopefully Ms. Dawson, her fifth grade teacher, wouldn't mind. She added some sauce and cheese to the noodles. Personally, she liked vacations in the summer time. She could go to the pool, hang out in the sun. With Thanksgiving just weeks away, she didn't consider this prime time to travel or play. But who was she to complain? "Where are we going?"

"Well, your aunt and uncle in Georgia invited us to have Thanksgiving with them. We thought, since we're going to be driving that far south, we would just make a trip of it and go to Florida, too. Maybe go to Disney World again."

Cassie stopped with a forkful of food almost in her mouth. Emily coughed on a swallow of water and sputtered, "Disney World? I've always wanted to go there!"

"Me too!" Scott said.

Even little Annette got involved, shouting, "Yeah, me too!"

"Well, everyone's been before except Annette," Mrs.

Jones reminded them all. "You just don't remember because you were little."

"I remember," Cassie said. "I remember lots of it." But the memories were hazy, foggy, like looking in the mirror after a shower. She couldn't be sure what was real and what was her imagination.

"I don't remember anything," Emily said.

"Don't expect it to be anything exciting," Mr. Jones said. "In fact, maybe we should just skip the whole Disney part. Really boring."

His statement was met with loud cries of dismay, and he grinned. "Or not. Then be sure and tell your teachers. We leave in a week."

"Wait, what about Scaredy?" Cassie said, her eyes widening in alarm as she thought about her dog. "We're not leaving him behind, are we?"

"Relax, honey," her mom said, patting her hand. "We have a sitter for both dogs and the cat."

Of course. Cassie nodded. She should have known they'd thought of that.

❤

"Disney World!" Danelle squealed. She handed her milk carton to Cassie, who always needed more milk at lunch. "That's so awesome! I've never been!"

"It's going to be cold," Riley said matter-of-factly. She primped her short, strawberry-blond hair with the palm of her hand and then picked up a sliver of bell pepper. "You won't have fun."

Cassie wrinkled her nose, both at the smell of the peppers

and at Riley's words. Danelle and Riley were her best friends and had been since she moved to Arkansas earlier this year. But the two girls didn't really like each other. As far as Cassie could tell, there was no real reason behind it, except that the dislike began in preschool and continued to this day. So Cassie always felt stuck in the middle, figuratively and sometimes literally.

"Those stink," she said, referencing the peppers.

Riley leaned closer to Cassie and took a big bite. "Mmm, yum."

Cassie pulled her head back. "How do you know it's cold? Have you been to Florida in November?"

"No. I don't want to, either. Sounds boring."

"Boring?" Danelle said, arching an eyebrow. A little bit heavier, Danelle was a complete opposite to Riley's petite frame. "Who doesn't want to go to Disney World? Oh, wait, I get it. You're jealous." She whispered loudly to Cassie, "Riley always acts this way when someone else is getting something she can't have."

Riley's cheeks turned beet red. Her nostrils flared, and Cassie knew she wanted to throw something at Danelle.

"Why don't you like Disney?" Cassie asked, trying to dig them out of the angry feelings swirling around them.

"It's for little kids," Riley snapped. "Are you a little kid?"

Danelle hooked an arm through Cassie's and tugged her toward her. "How would you know, Riley? It's not like you've ever even left Arkansas."

That intrigued Cassie. She and her family had moved here from Texas, so she had at least those two states under her belt. Not to mention all the other ones her family had visited. "Really? You've never been out of Arkansas?"

"Who cares?" Riley bit down hard on another pepper. "I've got everything I need right here."

Danelle huffed and mumbled something under her breath.

Riley stood up, holding her lunch tray close to her chest. "I'm done eating."

"I told you," Danelle said. "I told you she's annoying and immature. If she doesn't like something, she tries to make other people feel bad."

"How can you possibly know that?" Cassie shook her head. "You went to the same preschool. She's hardly the same person."

"Yeah? She seems the same to me." Danelle pulled a toothbrush out of her purse. She always brushed her teeth after lunch, or food got stuck in her braces. "I'm excited for you. Buy me something nice."

"Thanks, Danelle," Cassie said, glad at least one of her friends was happy for her. She didn't always understand Riley. They were in the same Girls' Club after school, and they got along great—most of the time. Sometimes it seemed Riley decided she couldn't stand Cassie anymore, or she was tired of her. And the mood swings often blind-sided her.

♥

Ms. Dawson approached Cassie on Friday with a stack of papers. "You said you'll be gone for a full week?"

Cassie looked at the papers and gulped. She gave an

apprehensive nod. "Yeah. Well, a week of school, and then the week of Thanksgiving. We start driving today." Ms. Dawson hadn't said anything about homework, and the closer it got to the end of the day, the more hopeful Cassie had become that there wouldn't be any.

"Well, I wrote down all of your assignments." She handed Cassie the top sheet, which had columns broken down into days, books, and page numbers. "That will get you through the week. And here are the worksheets you'll need to do." She placed the rest of the papers on Cassie's desk.

Cassie nodded, trying not to look too disappointed. There would be plenty of time on the drive down to Florida for her to work on this stuff.

"Have a blast!" Ms. Dawson said, giving her a smile. "We'll see you when you get back."

She said goodbye to her friends before she got on the bus, even though Riley had remained cool and distant all week.

"I'm serious!" Danelle said. "Bring me something cool!"

Cassie laughed and hoped Danelle wasn't that serious, because she didn't have money to buy things.

Her dad was home when the bus dropped Cassie and her siblings off. All doors and the trunk of the van were open as he loaded it up for the trip. "I need your suitcases," he said. "Put whatever you're going to use to entertain yourselves in the seats next to you. Don't forget pillows and sleeping bags."

Cassie retrieved her suitcase, packed the night before. She opened her fun bag and made sure it had everything she needed for a two-day drive. She had five of her favorite books, stencils, and a collection of brain-teaser puzzles. Cassie opened her backpack and added her homework to the fun bag.

The blanket on her bed moved, and Scaredy poked his head out. Cassie petted his nose, letting him lick her hand. "Don't forget me while I'm gone," she murmured.

She carried her things out to the car, then went back to her room to give Scaredy a big goodbye hug. "Be good for the babysitter. I'll see you when we get back!"

CHAPTER SIXTEEN
Car Trouble

It was a full two hours later before everyone was finally in the van. Mr. Jones was yelling, Emily was crying, Scott was complaining, and Mrs. Jones just put on her seat belt, leaned her head back, and shut her eyes.

They backed out of the driveway, and Mr. Jones launched into a tirade about being ready on time and following instructions. "This will be a lousy vacation if I have to yell at you kids every five minutes for not doing what I told you!" He made eye contact with every child in the rear-view mirror.

Nobody said anything for the first twenty minutes of the drive. Cassie entertained herself with her puzzles, and even felt some contentment at the thought of the hours in the car ahead of them.

Not Scott. "Why aren't we flying?" he asked, just half an hour into the trip. "It would be so much easier."

"Way too expensive," Cassie said, knowing the answer

before her father could say it. "Just going to Disney is expensive."

"And we're going to two different places," her dad said. "We'd have to fly to Florida and fly home from Georgia. Airlines don't like to do that."

Twenty minutes later Scott was grumbling again. "How much longer?"

"Well, we've been driving less than an hour," Mr. Jones said, an edge of irritation in his voice. "So we have about six hours left for today."

"That's too far!" Scott groaned.

Cassie wished desperately for some headphones. She could tell already this was going to be a long journey.

♥

The first day of driving was uneventful and dull. Cassie started out strong doing her homework, but after about half an hour, she tired of it.

They crossed over into Tennessee and then Mississippi. Cassie fanned herself, noting that it was warming up in the car. "Daddy," she said, "it's getting hot back here."

"Turn the AC on, Jim," Mrs. Jones said.

"You do it," he replied. "I'm driving."

A moment later the cooler air began to kick out of the vents above Cassie's seat. "Must be nice weather outside," she said.

"Must be," Emily agreed. "I see the sun shining."

They listened to an audio book and endured Scott's constant nagging before finally reaching a hotel around ten at night.

Nobody was excited the next morning as Mr. Jones marched them into the car around six a.m. "Just eleven more hours," her mom said as everyone got seated. As if that was supposed to be reassuring.

Cassie ate her morning pop tart and went back to sleep. When she woke up, two hours had passed. She immersed herself in her stencils, and then started reading her second book. When she finished it, she sighed and tossed it on the seat beside her. Nothing was fun right now, not even reading. "What's that smell?" she asked. At first she had thought it was someone's barbecue, but as it got stronger, it just smelled like something burning.

"Jim, pull over," her mom said, placing a hand on his arm and pointing out the window. Little puffs of smoke billowed up from the hood. Her dad grumbled something and Cassie sat up straighter, trying to see over her siblings' heads in the middle row.

"Is the car broken?" Emily asked.

"Let's hope not," Cassie said, consulting the watch on her wrist. They'd only been driving for five hours. They were nowhere near their final destination.

Mr. Jones got out of the car and propped the hood up. Cassie undid her seatbelt, and her mom whipped around.

"Do not get out of your seat!" she ordered.

Cassie made a face and redid her seatbelt. A few minutes later, her dad got back in.

"I think it's overheating," he said. "I need to get it to a mechanic to look at."

Her mom looked around, and Cassie did too. They were

on a highway somewhere in Georgia, with nothing around except thick trees, the colorful leaves still making their lazy descent from the upper branches to the ground. There weren't even any road signs or other cars driving around.

"Well, I guess we better pray it makes it to the next exit," Mrs. Jones sighed.

The next exit sign appeared ten minutes later, along with the words "No Services" written across the bottom. Mr. Jones put his blinker on, the steady *click click click* reaching all the way to the back of the car.

"Don't take that exit!" her mom snapped. "There's no services! We'll just waste our time driving around!"

He took of the blinker.

Five minutes later another sign appeared, this time with a few unrecognizable restaurants and gas stations listed.

"It's not really smoking anymore," Mr. Jones said. "Maybe it was just a piece of leaf or something that caught fire and had to burn off."

"If you think so," Mrs. Jones said.

"Yeah, I think we're good."

Cassie relaxed and pulled out another one of her books. She knew she should work on her homework, but that wasn't nearly as interesting as reading. "Crisis averted," she told Emily. "The car's fine."

"Are we there yet?" Scott asked from the middle row.

"I'm hungry!" Annette announced for the hundredth time.

"Cassie, snacks," her mom said.

Cassie leaned over and opened the big green cooler

between the two rows. "Grapes, anyone?"

As she handed out the green globes, she thought she smelled smoke again. She sniffed the air. "What's that smell?"

"Jim!" her mom exclaimed.

The tires squealed as the van veered to the right. Cassie grabbed onto Annette's chair as the car came to a screeching halt.

Without a word, her dad got out and rounded the car. Mrs. Jones sighed, and Cassie finished handing out the grapes. She sat back and watched her dad pop the hood. Small ribbons of smoke rose up around him.

He closed it and got back in the car. "Let's just sit for a bit," he said. "It needs to cool off."

This was definitely not fun. It was one thing to sit in a car for hours knowing they were getting closer to where they wanted to be; it was quite another to sit for hours and go nowhere.

Plus it was getting toasty in here. Cassie pushed up the sleeves of her shirt and fanned her face. Her mom rolled down the windows.

After about twenty minutes, Mr. Jones turned the engine on again. They sat for a few minutes, waiting for him to make his verdict. Cassie sniffed the air. She didn't smell any smoke this time. The engine emitted a deep hum, but otherwise seemed fine.

"All right, I think we're good." Her dad eased their way back onto the interstate.

"We have to get to a mechanic before we go home," Mrs.

Jones said.

"I know, I know. First thing tomorrow."

"How much longer?" Scott whined.

"Six more hours," Mrs. Jones said.

Six more hours. That would get them there around eight o'clock tonight. When they left the hotel, they'd hoped to get there a little before seven. Already lost an hour.

Cassie turned back to her book. She wiped her brow and realized she was sweating. "It's hot back here again."

"It's really hot, Jim," her mom said.

"Well, you want me to focus on driving, or making the car comfortable?"

She exhaled loudly and leaned over the controls. "It says the AC is on."

"Then it is."

Cassie put her hand up to the vent. "It's blowing air. It's just not cold."

Mrs. Jones punched a bunch of buttons. "It's not working."

"Has to be. It was working fine earlier."

"That was before the car started smoking, wasn't it?"

The two of them bickered back and forth. Cassie tried to tune them out and concentrate on her book. She didn't want to think about how hot it felt back here.

Mr. Jones pulled the van over, and Cassie looked up. "Why are we stopping?"

"The van's smoking again," Mrs. Jones muttered, pressing her fingers to the middle of her forehead. Cassie hoped she wasn't getting a headache.

They sat and waited the prescribed twenty minutes, and then her dad started the car up again.

It continued that way for the next several hours. They'd drive a half hour, one hour at the most, and stop when the car started smoking. The heat became unbearable, and her mom gave them permission to get out of the car when they stopped.

When they finally pulled into the campsite, it was after ten p.m. Cassie was hungry, hot, and grumpy.

"Let's get the tent up," Mr. Jones said, hauling out the large fabric bag.

"It's late," Cassie said, swatting at a mosquito. "Can't we just sleep in the RV?"

"No," he said. "This was the arrangement you wanted. You girls in the tent, us in the RV."

It had sounded like a fun idea last week, inside their chilly house in Arkansas. Now it sounded miserable. "We can put it up tomorrow. Right, Emily?"

"No, let's sleep in the tent," Emily said.

Cassie groaned. "Mom, I'm tired. I just want to lay down."

Her mom paused, the big green cooler in her arms. "Jim, just let them sleep in the RV tonight."

"But I don't want to!" Emily exclaimed.

"They don't want to," her dad echoed.

"I do!" Cassie said. But it didn't matter. Her dad and Emily had already started setting up the tent. Cassie blinked back tears of frustration and went to the car. She waited until the tent was up, then pulled out her sleeping bag and pillow.

"Good night, girls," her dad said. Everyone else was already in the RV, probably sleeping now, feeling the artificial cool air generated by the air conditioner. "See you in the morning."

Cassie crawled into the tent, fluffed her pillow, and didn't bother answering. What a miserable start to their vacation.

CHAPTER SEVENTEEN
Magic Time

"Well, I don't know what to tell you folks." The mechanic stuffed a greasy rag in the pocket of his overalls, then removed his baseball cap and scratched his balding head. "I don't see anything wrong with your car."

"Be quiet," Cassie told Scott and Annette for the hundredth time. She was trying to listen to her parents and the mechanic, but it was hard to hear over her brother and sister's giggling. They jumped around the old tires where her mom had left Cassie in charge. She grabbed Annette's arm as she ran by and yanked her down. "You're supposed to be sitting still!"

"There has to be something wrong," her dad was arguing. "All the way from Georgia, we were stopping to let it cool off because it was overheating. It doesn't take a mechanic to know that a car in good condition doesn't do that."

The man shrugged. "I'm sorry. I mean, you can leave it

here if you want. But other than maybe an oil change, I don't know what else we could do to it."

"Let's just go," her mom said, hands on her hips, a visor shielding her eyes from the bright Florida sun.

"Here." Mr. Jones paid the mechanic and gestured to the kids. Annette and Scott took off for the car.

"Come on, Emily," Cassie said, nudging her sister's foot. "We're finally going to Disney World."

"Yay," Emily said, putting her book away.

They pulled out onto the highway, following the big signs that beckoned them to the land of Mickey Mouse.

"So what happens if the car breaks down on the way home?" Cassie asked.

"We do what we did on the way here," her dad said shortly. "And take it to a real mechanic when we get home."

All of Cassie's concerns about the car faded away, however, as they approached the Disney gates. Familiar characters and princesses decorated the booths, and though Cassie didn't squeal or bounce in her seat like Annette, her pulse quickened in excitement.

"We're here!" Emily cheered.

"Yeah!" Scott yelled, and everyone joined him, even her mother.

They parked the car and got out, and Cassie couldn't take her eyes from the beautiful sculptured shrubs, or the long line of people waiting to get in.

"I want to see everything," she said, feeling her face split wide with a grin. "We can't miss anything."

"Don't worry, we'll see it all," her mom said.

"Where's the castle?" Emily asked. They followed the crowd of people, handing over their tickets. "I don't see anything."

"That's because we're not at the park," Mrs. Jones said. "We're at the station. From here we can take the monorail or the ferry to the Magic Kingdom."

"The mono-what?" Cassie asked. She didn't remember as much from the first visit as she'd thought. Everything looked unfamiliar and new. Then again, she'd only been four years old.

"The monorail," her mom said. "It's a train that connects the parks. We hop on the station here and can take the train to Magic Kingdom or to EPCOT, or even some of the hotels on Disney property."

"A train?" Scott's eyes looked ready to bug out of his head. "I wanna ride the train!"

"The train, the train, let's do the train!" Annette squealed.

"Yeah, that sounds fun," Cassie said, and Emily nodded.

"This way, then," Mr. Jones said, gesturing for them to follow him up the ramp. They stood in impatient anticipation as the monorail finally appeared in the distance, a train shaped more like a speeding bullet. It came to an abrupt stop in front of them, and all along the sides, doors slid open.

"This is awesome!" Emily giggled, climbing on.

After a moment, the doors closed, and the train sped off again. Scott stared when the tracks led them right through a building.

They arrived too soon for Annette and Scott. "Can we go

again?" Annette begged. "Please?"

"We will when the park closes," Mrs. Jones said.

"Guys, it's not even a ride," Cassie said, anxious to leave the station behind. "The real stuff's still in front of us. Look!" She pointed to Cinderella's castle, just looming in the distance. The blue towers stood out against the slate walls, and Cassie found herself wishing more than anything that she could climb those towers. She remembered fantasizing about being a princess when she was a little girl. Now here she was, all grown-up and still wanting to see the world from the top of a castle.

"Wait till you see Main Street," Mrs. Jones said. She and Mr. Jones exchanged a smile, and she took his hand.

They walked through the gates and came out in—a town? Cassie blinked in surprise at the quaint buildings nestled up against one another, a cobble street paving the way between them.

"Shops," her mother explained. "But isn't it beautiful?"

"Amazing!" Cassie said. Her gaze remained transfixed above her, staring at the decorate lettering over the doors. Candy shop, Barber shop, toy shop, holiday shop, bakery, ice-cream shop. Her stomach rumbled appreciatively. "Let's get started!"

♥

The lines weren't too bad this time of year, but the Joneses still had to deal with some wait time. Cassie's favorite was the dwarf mine ride, a little roller coaster that played through the scenes of "Snow White." Annette liked "The Little Mermaid" ride the most.

For lunch they ate at Geppetto's Workshop, a cafe made to look like it came out of the "Pinocchio" movie. Maybe Cassie was just starving, but she thought the soup in a bread bowl was phenomenal. She ate every last bit, savoring the bowl after the soup was gone.

"Magic Kingdom closes at seven," Mr. Jones said, spreading his map out across the table. "And there's a lot to see. I suggest we make an orderly trek through this part of the park, and when we run out of time, we hop on the monorail and head to EPCOT."

"Yeah, the monorail!" Annette said.

"What time does EPCOT close?" Cassie asked, sitting up straight and looking at the map with her father.

"Nine o'clock. And they have a really fun fireworks show that you kids will probably like."

"We better get going," Mrs. Jones said. "Time's ticking."

The next few hours flew by. Her dad gathered them up before the crowds started and herded them to EPCOT, where Cassie had the best chocolate mousse with raspberry sauce she'd ever had in her life.

"Norway, huh?" she said, taking her last bite of mousse. "I'll have to go visit someday."

By the time she crawled into her tent that night, she couldn't care less where she was sleeping. Her whole mind buzzed with a happy energy, but her body collapsed in exhaustion. *What a perfect day*, she thought.

CHAPTER EIGHTEEN
Rainy Days

Cassie dreamed she was swimming. She knew it was dream because never would she go swimming in all her clothes, and in her dream she was sopping wet in a shirt and jeans. She dove into the pool and came out shivering. She picked up a towel to dry off, but it was wet too.

"I can't get warm!" she said to no one. Her teeth chattered with the cold.

"Cassie."

Cassie opened her eyes to see the dark shadow of Emily above her, shaking her shoulders. "Cassie, wake up."

"What's wrong, Emily?" she murmured. Abruptly she realized how cold she was. And wet. No wonder she'd been dreaming about swimming.

"It's raining and the tent's soaking. What should we do?"

Cassie sat up, hearing now the tinkling of the rain as it fell on the canvas. Moisture gathered in small drops on the inside of the fabric, dropping on them when gravity became too difficult to resist. Water seeped into the tent from the ground, and the sleeping bags were drenched.

"Argh!" Cassie exclaimed. She picked up her bag of clothes, hoping something inside would be dry. "Let's get in the RV!"

Emily grabbed her stuff too and both girls tumbled out of the tent. Cassie protected her head with her bag and rapped on the RV door. "Mom!" she shouted.

"Daddy!" Emily added.

No response, and Cassie banged harder. The rain continued to pour around them, and she trembled. "Mother!" she hollered.

The door opened, and Mr. Jones stood in the doorway,

the RV dark behind him.

"Come in, come in," he murmured, his voice thick with sleep.

"Gotta get out of these clothes," Cassie said. Her father vanished into the bathroom and came back with towels.

"What's going on?" Mrs. Jones asked, coming out of the back bedroom.

"It's raining and the girls are wet." He looked around the RV. The couch was already made into a bed, and Scott and Annette slept there. "I think the table folds out."

Cassie found a dry shirt and pants to put on. By the time she finished getting dressed, her dad had the table made into a bed. It was small for the two girls, but it was dry. "Change, Emily," Cassie said to her sister, who still stood there in her sopping clothes. Half asleep, Emily started changing.

Mrs. Jones went back to the bedroom, but Mr. Jones waited until they had crawled into the bed. "Are you warm?" he asked.

Cassie fluffed the towel under her head and nodded, tiredness pulling at her eyes and making her head feel heavy. "Yeah."

"Mm-hmm," Emily agreed.

"Good. We'll see you in the morning, then."

♥

The rain had lessened by morning, the steady downpour replaced by a gloomy drizzle. The temperature had dropped as well, and Mrs. Jones made everyone wear sweaters under their rain jackets.

"It was so warm yesterday," Cassie said, wrapping the

sweater around her. "How did it get cold?"

"It's November here, too," her mom said, zipping Annette's jacket. "It might not get as cold, but the weather certainly cools off."

The entry gates with the colorful Disney characters greeted them, cheerful even in the cloudy mist.

"Can we take the monorail again?" Scott asked.

"No," Cassie said, still determined to try everything at least once. "Today we need to take the ferry!"

"Fairies are for girls!" Scott said.

"I love fairies!" Annette said.

"Not that kind of fairy," Emily said. "A ferry like a boat."

"It's a boat?" Scott asked, still looking uncertain.

"Yep," Cassie said.

"I guess that's fine, then," Scott muttered, looking down at the toy transformer in his hands like he didn't want to admit he was pleased.

It was cold. Cassie shivered as they got out of the van. She wanted the warm sunshine from yesterday. They got on the ferry and moved to the front. A little girl about Cassie's age sat on a bench, her hands clutched around her father's arm. Cassie gave her a smile and the girl smiled back. She leaned toward her dad and said something that Cassie didn't understand at all.

Cassie sat next to her father and tried to eavesdrop on their conversation, but no matter how she strained her ears, the words didn't make sense to her. "Are they speaking another language?" she asked her dad.

"They're speaking Spanish," he said. Then Mr. Jones

turned to the man and said something. The two conversed in Spanish for a bit.

"Cassie," Mr. Jones said, taking her hand and pulling her in front of him, "say, '*Como te llamas?*'"

Cassie looked at him, not sure she could repeat those sounds.

"*Como te llamas*," he repeated. "Say it to the little girl."

Cassie forced a smiled and pronounced, "*Como te llamas*?"

"*Maria*," the girl said. Her black eyes glittered when she smiled. "*Como te llamas*?"

Cassie turned to her father, not sure what to say now.

"She just told you her name," he said. "And then she asked yours. Answer her."

"Cassie," she said.

The girl said something else, the separation of the vowels and consonants completely lost on Cassie.

"What did she say now?" she asked.

"Ask her," her father prodded.

Cassie sat back down, flustered and embarrassed. "I don't understand Spanish."

"She said, 'nice to meet you.'" Mr. Jones said something to the father, and the two men laughed.

Cassie didn't try to speak again, but she listened to the exchange between them. They said goodbye when they got off the ferry.

"She seemed nice," Cassie said.

"You should have tried to talk to her more. She was excited to talk to someone."

"I don't speak Spanish."

"I could teach you."

Cassie considered that. "It's a very pretty language. It all blends together, kind of sing-songy. Sounded like they were singing."

"Yes, you're right. Spanish does sound like a song."

Cassie paid more attention after that. She noticed several times when she thought she heard people speaking Spanish, and other times when she couldn't tell what language it was. Maybe someday she'd have to learn another language.

♥

No one took any chances on the rain that night. Mrs. Jones spent the last hours of the evening at the laundromat, drying the sleeping bags for Emily and Cassandra. Then the girls joined the rest of the family in the RV, warm and cozy on their table-turned-bed.

"What was your favorite part about today?" Cassie whispered. She could hear Annette and Scott breathing deeply at their end of the RV. They had fallen asleep almost as soon as they laid down.

"The Japanese restaurant," Emily whispered back. "I love watching them cut up and cook our food. And it's the first time I've eaten with chopsticks."

"Yeah, that was awesome," Cassie agreed. So far, the food had been one of the highlights of the vacation. As long as she had good food to eat, she was happy.

"What about yours?" Emily asked.

"I don't know. Maybe meeting Maria." Even though she hadn't been able to talk to the girl, she hadn't been able to get her off her mind. "I wish I had a way to talk to her some more. I should have gotten her address. We could be penpals."

"Maybe you'll see her tomorrow," Emily murmured. Her words slurred together as her mouth grew too tired to open.

"Yeah, maybe," Cassie said, but she doubted it. Tomorrow they were going to the water park, and she had a feeling it would be cold. She suspected her family would be the only one crazy enough to be there.

But even if she didn't see Maria, she liked the idea of a penpal. She decided to meet someone else from another country and exchange addresses. What fun it would be to get mail from somewhere outside of America.

CHAPTER NINETEEN

Abandon Tent

The water park didn't open as early as the other parks, so the Jones family ate breakfast inside the trailer.

"The sun's out," Mrs. Jones said, putting the milk back in the refrigerator.

"That doesn't mean it's warm," Mr. Jones said, sounding grumpy. "It's about sixty-five degrees outside."

"Is that cold?" Cassie asked.

"It's warmer than yesterday," her mom said. "Do you not want to go, Jim?"

"I never said that." Mr. Jones put on a baseball cap and walked out of the trailer.

"Is he mad?" Cassie asked.

"Just tired. Vacations wear on him."

Cassie couldn't understand that. She was tired, but vacations were fun, weren't they?

♥

Cassie loved swimming. She could spend all day at the

pool, doing nothing but underwater handstands and splashing around.

By the time they got to the water park, however, it had started to rain again. She stood under the cabana her mom had claimed, teeth chattering as she shivered out of her shirt and placed it on the table.

"But it's raining," Scott was saying as he clutched his towel to his chest.

"And you're going to get in the water. You'll be wet anyway. Stop complaining." Mr. Jones pulled Scott's shirt over his head. "If no one wants to be here, we'll just pack up and head back right now."

"No, no, we want to be here," Cassie said. She rubbed her bare shoulders, trying to erase the goosebumps popping out all along her arms. "The lazy river looks fun. Come on, guys." She forced herself to walk away from her towel, though she was so cold her body ached.

"Cassie, keep Annette with you." Mrs. Jones gave Annette a little shove, and Annette's skinny legs ran her over to Cassie. She had on her floaties.

"Stick close by," Cassie told her. "I don't want to lose you."

"We're like the only ones here," Emily murmured, grabbing an empty intertube and handing it to Cassie.

"But not quite. See? There's people." She pointed to two teenage boys a ways ahead of them on the river. Cassie put Annette in the tube and climbed up beside her. Both of them lifted their legs up, keeping as few body parts in the water as possible.

Scott and Emily got in their own tube and pushed off behind Cassie.

She couldn't get warm. She shivered and rubbed her arms. Her teeth chattered, and she cringed anytime the water touched her. She looked at Annette, her lips trembling and blue.

This isn't fun, Cassie thought.

A tunnel appeared up ahead, with a waterfall flowing across the opening. Cassie groaned. The only way onward was through the water. She tried to push the intertube to one side so they wouldn't get as wet, but the resulting cascade didn't seem any less than it would have been. The dark tunnel was even colder than the open air, and Annette began to cry.

"It's okay," Cassie told her. She touched her sister's freezing skin. "We'll be out soon."

Nobody said a word as they reached an exit to the lazy river. All four of them ascended the steps. Cassie imagined her expression matched the grim faces she saw on her brother and sisters.

"I just want to dry off and go home," Emily said.

"We should at least try the slides," Cassie said, not quite ready to give up on the day. "Don't they look fun?"

Annette's teeth clattered together, the remnants of tears in the corners of her eyes. "N-n-no."

"I'll go with you," Scott said.

"I can't leave Annette."

"I'll take her back to Mom," Emily said. "We'll sit and wait."

"Okay." Cassie started for the tall slides, wishing the sun would come out. Even for just a little bit. It would make all the difference in the day.

They climbed to the top of the platform, following the small line of other people who hadn't realized how cold it would be today. A wind blew across them, and Cassie couldn't stop shaking. She felt like she'd never be warm again.

Scott went first, and Cassie watched him disappear with the first dip in the slide. She sat down in the shallow pool at the top. The frigid water tickled her thighs, promising more icy delights to come. She could chicken out, get up and go back down the steps.

"Your turn," the boy running the slide line said.

Just get it over with. Cassie sucked in a breath and pushed off. Instantly the air pressure knocked her against the slide. She crossed her arms over her chest, helpless as the water splashed her face, her arms, her neck, places that she had managed to keep dry up until now. Then the slide ended, and she plunged into a pool of water. She shot her feet down and found the bottom, then pushed her head out with a gasp and a sputter.

Scott waited for her at the side. He took her arm and helped her out. Cassie shook from head to toe.

"All right," she said between clenched teeth. "I think I'm done."

❤

The only thing everyone wanted to do after the water park was take a nice, hot shower. Mrs. Jones refused to let everyone use the tiny shower, so Mr. Jones led them down the trail to the shower house closest to the RV.

Cassie stayed in the shower longer than necessary. The hot water steamed up in the stall and billowed around her. She closed her eyes and waved it in her face, inhaling the misty warmth. Slowly the cold infused in her bones started to peel away.

"Cassie?" Emily called. "Annette went back with Daddy. I'm supposed to wait for you. Are you almost done?"

She did not want to be done. But the shampoo was out of her hair, and her body no longer felt cold. She turned the water off and counted to five before opening the stall door. The chilly air blasted over her, and she jerked the towel around her body, rubbing her skin and drying off as quickly as possible.

"Should we sleep in the tent tonight?" Emily asked.

Cassie pulled on her pajamas. "No way. I only just got warm again."

"Yeah. Me too."

They trooped back to the RV, where Mrs. Jones was setting the table for dinner.

"Mom," Cassie said, "I don't think it's a good idea if we sleep outside. It might rain, and everything will get wet again."

"That's fine," her mom said. "Just sit down and eat."

♥

Cassie woke up in the morning to see her dad emptying the cupboards and packing things up. She rubbed her eyes and sat up. "That went by fast."

"Yep," he said. "Vacations usually do. Next stop, your cousins' house."

Cassie waited her turn to use the bathroom, then packed up her clothes. Her backpack fell on the floor, and she paused to examine it. The heavy text books inside reminded her of all the homework she hadn't yet done. "I'll do it on the drive to Georgia," she promised. She headed outside to help load up the van.

The day looked like it would be warmer than the previous two. Already the air held the promise of heat, the little teasing kiss that made her want to shed her sweater. The sun crowned on the horizon.

"Looks like we went to the water park on the wrong day," she said to Emily, joining her at the van.

"I hated yesterday," Emily said. "I wish we'd gone back to Disney World."

"Yeah. But we didn't have any more tickets." It hadn't been enough. She hoped they'd come again and stay longer next time.

CHAPTER TWENTY
Thanksgiving

Cassie held her breath the whole way to Georgia that the car would make it. Surprisingly, it didn't start smoking once. Maybe the mechanic had been right and there really wasn't anything wrong with it.

It was late evening by the time they arrived. They parked in the long driveway, and before Cassie even had the chance to get out of the car, her cousins spilled out the side door. She'd seen them a few years ago at a family reunion, but she couldn't remember their names. She climbed over the cooler and got out.

"Hi," she said to the girl. "I'm Cassie."

"I know who you are," she replied. "You're my cousin."

Yes, but Cassie was drawing a blank as to her name. "And you're. . . ?"

"Carla," she said with a scoff. "You don't remember our names?"

All three of them stared at her now, and Cassie glanced

around for her mom. But her parents had gone into the house, their arms laden with luggage. "Sure, I remember. You've just changed, and I wasn't sure who was who."

"Oh, okay." That seemed to satisfy her. "Bring in your stuff, and I'll show you where you're sleeping."

Cassie got her sleeping bag and duffel bag. After a moment's hesitation, she grabbed her backpack. She'd only spent about half an hour on her homework today. She'd probably have the chance to do more here.

"Everyone can come," Carla said, directing her siblings to help get bags. "You're all sleeping in the same place."

"Okay," Cassie said. She nodded at Emily. "Emily, Annette, Scott, come on." She followed Carla into the garage and up a set of stairs, then through the kitchen and into a big room on the other side.

"This is where y'all will be sleeping," Carla said.

Cassie dumped her sleeping bag against the wall. Two big televisions faced the room. "What do you usually do in here?"

"It's the game room. The boys play video games on that screen and we watch movies on that one." She pointed out the different screens. "The boys will probably be in tomorrow morning to play. This is where they hang out."

"Oh. Great." Cassie nodded. "Thanks."

"Yeah. We'll see you in the morning." Carla backed out of the room.

One of the boys who looked a little younger than Scott was showing off a toy.

"That's awesome!" Scott said. "Does it transform?"

Cassie hid a smile. Scott wanted everything to transform.

"No. It's not a transformer. I have a great video game, though. I'll show you tomorrow."

"I love video games!"

Not Cassie. Big waste of time, if anyone asked her. She hadn't gotten a great "welcome" vibe from Carla. Cassie had a sudden longing for her own bed, her own room, her own dog. She unrolled her sleeping bag and curled up inside.

♥

Boring.

That was the best word to describe hanging out at Carla's house.

The younger boy invaded the guest room before Cassie was even awake, turning on the video game. The gaming started before breakfast and showed no signs of stopping.

Cassie got dressed and ate cereal. At least they had a good selection. Her aunt and uncle were there, but no sign of Carla or her brother.

"Where's Carla?" Cassie asked, putting her dirty bowl in the sink.

"Around here, we take care of our dirty dishes," her uncle Gary said, stopping her before she left the sink. "You need to put your bowl in the dishwasher."

"Oh." Cassie blushed under the chastisement and retrieved her dirty bowl. She carefully lined it up in the dishwasher. She was almost afraid to ask again, but she did anyway. "Where's Carla?"

Her uncle walked out of the kitchen, and her aunt said,

"Probably in her room."

"Thanks," Cassie said, and she hurried away, wondering why her mom's relatives were so weird.

She had never been upstairs before but figured Carla's room must be up there, since nothing else was down here. She ran into her parents in the front room, sitting and reading.

"Hi," she said, joining them.

"Hi, dear," her mom said, putting a book down. "Why aren't you with Carla?"

"I think she's still sleeping," Cassie said. "I haven't seen her yet today."

"Well, go play. Once we start making food for Thanksgiving, you won't have the chance to hang out."

Go play. Such great advice. If only she could find something to do. "Okay." She climbed the stairs and paused at the top. A bathroom and three closed doors faced her. She knocked on one door and pushed it open.

"This is my office," her uncle said, not even turning around in his leather chair. He sat with his back to her, typing away at a computer. "There's a game room downstairs and a living room and a library. Find somewhere else to play."

Cassie closed the door quietly, not bothering responding. She felt like a nuisance in this house. She gave up looking for Carla's room and went back to the guest room. With nothing else to do, she pulled out her backpack and selected a homework assignment.

How utterly shameful, when she was resigned to do

homework for entertainment.

♥

Nobody gathered for a formal lunch. Cassie wandered into the kitchen when she got hungry, and her mom made her a sandwich. Then she put her to work peeling potatoes.

"Did you find Carla?" she asked.

"No," Cassie replied. She didn't elucidate on the situation, either. She peeled potatoes, then peeled sweet potatoes, then helped roll out pie crusts. Slowly, her spirits began to rise. Tomorrow was Thanksgiving. She couldn't complain.

Her aunt prepared a quick meal of soup and crackers for dinner, and Mrs. Jones rounded up her kids. Cassie still hadn't seen Carla all day.

"Are your kids coming to dinner?" she asked Aunt Jadene.

Her aunt handed her a stack of bowls. "Put these on the table, please," she said. Then she walked over to a speaker in the wall and pressed a button. "Kids, we're eating dinner. Time to come down."

Cassie stared in fascination at the wall. "Is that an intercom?"

"Yes." Her aunt took the bowls from her and began to place them on the table. "It's quieter and more efficient than yelling." She gave Mrs. Jones a significant look.

"It works just fine in our house," Mrs. Jones said with a shrug. "Right, Cassie?"

Cassie much preferred everything about their house, all the way down to the endless amounts of noise. "I like it."

Aunt Jadene laughed. "Boy, you've got them trained, Karen."

At least we don't spend all day in our rooms, Cassie thought, but she said nothing. Especially when Carla and her brother trooped into the kitchen a moment later, disgruntled expressions on their faces. Scott and Annette came out of the game room with the youngest.

They said a blessing over the soup and started eating.

"What have you done all day?" Cassie asked Carla.

"Just listened to music and written in my journal. It's been a nice, relaxing day."

"You should play with your cousins while they're here," Aunt Jadene said. "They won't be here forever, you know."

Carla looked at her mother and rolled her eyes. Her expression was easy to interpret: the sooner they're gone, the better.

Cassie couldn't have said it better herself.

♥

She spent Thanksgiving Day in the game room, learning how to play video games with her boy cousins. She was horrible at it. Even the youngest at three years old was way better than Cassie. And they had no patience with her. Instead of giving her instructions on what to do better, they just yelled at her and told her to give them the controller.

Cassie only too willingly obliged them. She worked on her homework until her mom yelled, "Time to eat!" The intercom in the room buzzed with Aunt Jadene's voice: "Dinner is ready, everyone."

Cassie dumped her homework and scurried out of the

room. Another table had been set up to accommodate all the food, and her mouth watered as she took it all in. There were her favorites, the must-haves at Thanksgiving: turkey, gravy, mashed potatoes, rolls. And a few items her aunt had added that she wasn't too sure about. And then, of course, the deserts: pumpkin pie, apple pie, cranberry pie, cherry pie. Cassie sat on her hands to keep from clapping.

"Before we eat," Mr. Jones said, coming up behind his wife and placing his hands on her shoulders, "we have a tradition in my family, if we may."

"Please," Uncle Gary said, motioning him forward.

"We always hand out to corn kernels." Her dad produced a small jar full of unpopped popcorn. "Everyone take two."

He started with Uncle Gary. Carla looked at them suspiciously, but took two, just like everyone else.

Cassie knew what was coming. She took her two and beamed at her father. Now it felt more like home.

"Now I'm going to pass the jar around again, and you're going to put the kernels back. But as you do, say one thing you are grateful for with each kernel."

Cassie didn't pay much attention to everyone else's gratitude lists. She formulated her two in her mind, wanting to say something impactful, true, and profound. The jar appeared in front of her, and she dropped one in.

"I'm grateful to live in a country where we can safely travel whenever we want." She dropped in the other. "And I'm grateful for a family that understands me and supports me." *And I understand them.* She looked at her mother and smiled, ever so glad to be a Jones.

Episode 4: Fever Pitch

CHAPTER TWENTY-ONE
Music on the Mind

Cassie ran the quarter of a mile from the bus stop to her house as fast as she could. Christmas was over, but the cold lingered, an unwelcome guest that would not leave.

She opened the front door and rushed inside, dropping her gloves and hat in a pile. "Ahh!" she exclaimed.

Her younger brother and sister burst in behind her, also shivering and shaking from the relentless cold. "I can't take it anymore!" Emily cried.

"Me neither," Cassie said. She trooped into the kitchen and put her backpack on the table. "Mom?"

"In the laundry room!" her mom called back. "Where did you put your gloves?"

Cassie knew what her mom was really saying: put your things away.

As the oldest of the four Jones children, she felt a certain pressure to set the right example. Sometimes she resented that feeling, but other times she appreciated the trust her parents showed her. Returning to the entry way, she picked up the discarded winter wear and threw it into the hall closet.

"It's too cold," she could hear Emily saying from the kitchen. "Can't you pick us up from the bus stop?"

"Or at least take us in the morning," Cassie said, joining the conversation. She took her turquoise-framed glasses off and wiped the moisture from them. They always fogged up when she came into a warm house from the cold.

Mrs. Jones looked up from the laundry. "It's good for you. When else do you run?"

Running? Since when was that the goal? "I don't like running," Cassie said. "I do it every day before recess. I hate it." She picked up an apple. "Do we have any brownies left?"

Her mom frowned at her. "No. But a brownie isn't a good snack. Just eat that apple."

Cassie took a big bite from it, trying to pretend the fruit had a chocolate flavor. It didn't work. She set it aside and focused on her mom. A driving thought had been pushing at her brain all morning, and she couldn't wait to bring it up to her mother. "Mom, I want to do something with music."

Mrs. Jones hauled the basket of clothes into the living room and beckoned Cassie to follow. "Oh? What do you mean?"

Cassie sat down to help fold the towels. "I don't know. In school, when we were practicing songs for the Christmas program, the music made me so happy. I wanted to spend all day singing. Now it's over, and I miss it."

"Well, do you want to do something with piano?"

Ugh, no. "I don't think so." She'd taken piano lessons for a year in Texas and hated it. Every practice had been agonizing, and she doubted she'd been very nice to the piano teacher. "It's pretty boring. Besides, my fingers lack dexterity."

"Dexterity?" Her mom giggled. "You're funny. Give me that towel before you rip it from folding it so often."

Cassie handed it over. "What other instruments could I play?"

"Well, I don't know. I've never played any." Mrs. Jones frowned as she considered the situation. "But you know what, your dad has played just about everything. Why don't you ask him when he gets home?"

"Sure," Cassie said, brightening. She grabbed her backpack from the kitchen table and went to her room, humming a song from the Christmas program they'd put on last month.

❤

"So how was everyone's day?" Mr. Jones looked around the table during dinner. "Annette?"

"Great," four-year-old Annette said, her standard answer to just about everything. Except when she said it, it sounded like, "Grape."

"Scott?"

He shrugged his shoulders. "Fine." Also the standard answer.

Mr. Jones took a bite from his meatball and then shook

his fork at Scott. "Remember what we talked about? You need to use your descriptive words to answer the question."

Scott sighed. "I was on yellow and missed five minutes of recess. But it wasn't my fault. Miles was loud at lunch and I just couldn't help it." He raised his eyebrows and shook his head to express his helplessness.

Cassie rolled her eyes. Scott might only be in the first grade, but he had the conniving mentality of a con artist.

"Well, tomorrow you'll stay on green, right?" Mr. Jones said.

"Right," he grumbled.

"Emily?"

"Perfect," she spouted, a smile on her lips. "I got a one-hundred percent on my spelling test. And Ms. Wright selected me to present for the third-grade assembly."

"That's great, Emily!"

Cassie forced herself to stab her food and stick in her mouth instead of making a negative comment. Emily excelled at everything she put her hand to. Of course she got perfect scores and was chosen to represent her class. Every day was roses and unicorns for Emily.

"And you, Cassie?"

Finally, her turn. Cassie adjusted her glasses on her nose and faced her dad. "I want to start playing an instrument, Daddy."

"Oh, really?" His graying eyebrows rose above the piercing blue eyes. "What kind of instrument?"

"I really don't know. Mom thought you could help me

choose."

He nodded, a sparkle of excitement in his eyes. "Well, let's see. I played the saxophone, the clarinet, the piano, even the drums for a bit."

"The clarinet sounds like fun."

"Can I play one?" Emily asked. "I want to play the clarinet also."

Cassie felt a flash of irritation and rounded on Emily, next to her at the table. "You already play the piano! You don't need another instrument." Though Cassie had bored of piano and moved on, Emily had taken to it like a fish in water. She was in the middle of her third year and mastering piano pieces that Cassie couldn't even pronounce.

"Why not? Daddy played lots of different ones."

So he had. Cassie glared at him for revealing that. "Can't this just be my thing?"

"I want to do the drums," Scott said. "That's what boys do, right? The drums?"

"Hang on, hang on." Mr. Jones threw his hands up and leaned back in his chair. "I think we might be on to something. How many other kids in the school do you think would love to play an instrument?"

Cassie had really no idea. She blinked and waited for her father to finish his thought.

"Let's say most of them. They'd have this same conversation at dinner, and most of them would want to play."

She drummed her fingers on the table, still waiting for

the point.

"So what if. . . ." He pointed a finger at Mrs. Jones and grinned. "What if I started a band?"

CHAPTER TWENTY-TWO
Dad's Band

"A band?" Mrs. Jones echoed carefully. "How would you do that?"

"Well, I'd have to get permission from the school, of course. But we could meet at the school, in the choir room a few times a week." Mr. Jones rubbed his hands together, grinning like a toddler at Easter. "This could work."

"You work full-time, Jim," Mrs. Jones said, a note of impatience in her voice. "When do you have time?"

"Well, there's before work, or after work. There's always a way, Karen." Her father's tone matched her mom's, a touch of irritation that she wasn't as excited as he was.

"I think it's a great idea!" Cassie threw in. She was already thinking about what fun it would be to have a band at school, and have her dad in charge, no less!

"I'll talk to Ms. King tomorrow," he said. "Why don't I drive you guys to school?"

"Yes!" Emily exclaimed.

Cassie grinned. They wouldn't have to ride the bus tomorrow. Or stand in the freezing weather while they waited for it to come. Things were already looking up.

♥

Cassie sat in her fifth-grade class, copying down the morning warm-ups from the board, when the intercom made the staticky sound that indicated the announcements were about to come on.

"Attention, please," the voice began. Cassie kept working. She could listen and get stuff done at the same time. Most of the announcements wouldn't apply to her, anyway. Reminders about car riders and walkers, sign ups for some activity.

"In addition to the Just Say No club, next week we are proud to announce that we will be starting a band."

Cassie put her pencil down and straightened. Her dad had been so excited after he talked to Ms. King, but he hadn't been sure the administration would approve his band. They must have told him yes!

"It will be under the direction of Jim Jones and will meet every Friday morning at seven a.m. in the music room. Fourth graders and above are invited to join."

No third graders. Cassie felt a guilty twinge of satisfaction. Emily wouldn't be able to join.

"Please bring any instrument of your choice. Instruments will not be provided for you. If you have any questions, please contact Ms. King."

Cassie's hand shot into the air.

"Not now, Cassie," Ms. Dawson said. "We're listening to

the announcements."

Cassie heaved a sigh of frustration and hunkered down in her chair. A moment later they all stood for the Pledge of Allegiance, and then the intercom clicked off.

"All right, everyone has five more minutes to finish up their warm-ups."

Cassie lifted her hand again, sitting up very straight in her chair.

"Yes, Cassandra, you have a question?"

"That's my dad's band," she said importantly. "He started it. He's the director."

"Well, that's very nice, Cassie."

"I'll be joining it," she continued. "It was my idea. I'm going to play the clarinet."

"Can't wait to hear you play. Anyone have any questions about the board work?"

Matthew Grace, the boy who had sat near Cassie all year, leaned toward her. "I've always wanted to be in a band. I think that's so cool. Can I bring my keyboard?"

"Sure!" Cassie said. "My dad said any instrument." She glanced around to see if anyone else wanted to ask her about the band, but the other students were concentrating on the assignment.

"Are you going to join the band?" she asked her best friend Riley at recess.

"I don't think anyone will want to drive me to school that early," she said. "And I don't have an instrument."

For a moment she thought about asking her other friend, Danelle, if she was coming. But Danelle hadn't really spoken to her since they started up again after Christmas. Cassie shrugged it off. There'd be other kids she knew. She could hardly wait for Friday. It would be so much fun.

♥

"I'm home!" Mr. Jones called, coming in the front door.

"Hi, Daddy," Cassie said as he came into the kitchen. She didn't even look up from where she unloaded the dishwasher.

"What happened to all my little children that used to come running to my arms?" he asked, pausing to give her a hug.

"We grew up?"

"Daddy!" As if on cue, little Annette rounded the corner into the kitchen. She threw her arms around his legs and grinned up at him.

"Guess what?" Cassie said, putting the last knife away in the drawer. "They announced your band today in school. Said it starts Friday. I'm so excited! I can't wait!"

He smiled. "Well, that's fantastic news, because look what I've got here." He led her back into the dining room, where what looked like two small suitcases sat under the piano bench. Her dog Scaredy sniffed them, then curled up around one and went to sleep.

"What are they?" Cassie asked, a niggle of excitement sprouting in her chest.

Her dad knelt and opened one up. The case was velvet lined, with small cylinder pieces fitted inside. "A clarinet. Let me show you how to put it together."

"Wow." A smile stretched across her face. She watched

her dad connect the cylinders until he had a long tube. "Where did you get it?"

"I'm renting it from someone at church."

She looked at the other case. "What's in that one?"

"Another clarinet."

"Oh." She frowned as a suspicion darkened her mind. "Do I need two?"

He chuckled as he connected the mouthpiece. "No. It's for Emily."

"But—but they said in morning announcements that it's only for fourth grade and up. Emily's in third."

"Ah, yes." Mr. Jones handed her the completed clarinet. "But as the band director, I am entitled to certain privileges."

So Emily got to be in the band, too. And she'd play the clarinet. Cassie accepted the instrument, a hollowness in her chest. Couldn't she have one thing that was her own? Just once? "Is Scott coming to? Playing the drums?"

"No." He shook his head. "First grade is too young. Scott couldn't sit still long enough to learn a beat. But Emily's a very advanced third-grader. I'm sure she'll do great." He nodded at the clarinet in her hands. "Don't you want to try it?" he asked, oblivious to the change in her mood.

"No, that's all right." Cassie handed it back. "I'll wait until Friday with everyone else. Thanks for getting it."

♥

Emily kept up a constant stream of excited conversation the whole drive to school on Friday. Cassie was grateful to be in a warm car, though they'd had to leave the house super early to get to practice on time. And her stomach tumbled over and around itself with nerves. She wished now that she'd let her dad give her some instruction before band started. What if everyone could play but her? What if she just wasn't very good?

They were the first ones in the music room, but it wasn't quite seven a.m. yet. Her dad set up a music stand and placed pictures around the room of different instruments.

"Let's have you girls sit over here," he said, directing Emily and Cassie to a spot on one side of the room.

"What if we're the only ones that come?" Cassie asked.

"You won't be," her dad said, looking quite satisfied with himself. "I had several parents call and verify the information. We should have a good crowd." He showed her and Emily how to put their clarinets together.

They had just finished when a few more kids walked in, toting various instruments of all sizes. Cassie recognized Konner Lane, a kid from one of the other fifth grade classes. He carried with him a small set of drums.

"Hi," Cassie said. "I'm in Ms. Dawson's class."

"Hi," he replied without quite meeting her eyes. He then moved to the farthest end of the music room and set up his drums.

Cassie frowned, then shrugged it off. Who really understood boys? Maybe he didn't want to be friends. She waited to see if Matthew would show up with his keyboard, but he didn't.

"All right, let's get started," her dad boomed, raising his hands behind the music stand in the center of the room.

"I'm Mr. Jones. I'm also Cassie and Emily's dad." He waved at them. "Everyone should have their instruments assembled by now, yes?" He glanced around, and no one contradicted him. "Let's see what you know. Everyone, hit middle C."

Hit what? Cassie glanced around as the kids fumbled with their instruments. Emily put her fingers on the clarinet and blew a note. Varying sounds began to screech out of the other instruments, very few of them matching the note Emily blew.

Cassie put her mouth on the reed and blew, frustration boiling up inside her. She didn't even know what middle C sounded like, and definitely didn't know where to find it on the clarinet. Wasn't her dad going to teach her? Of course Emily knew. She played piano. She knew everything about music.

Her dad walked around the room, repositioning hands, tightening strings. He got to Cassie and moved her fingers to press different buttons. She pulled the clarinet from her mouth.

"I don't know how to play the clarinet. You have to teach me where middle C is."

"I am teaching you," he replied, and walked away.

CHAPTER TWENTY-THREE
A Little Under

One thing was very clear after band practice: Cassie was one of the only kids who walked in not having a clue how to play their instrument. She'd never even put it in her mouth until that day.

Some of the kids stored their instruments in the closet, but Cassie carried her clarinet home. She had one task this weekend: learn how to play.

She reassembled it in the dining room, checking to make sure she had all the parts right. She picked up the reed and hesitated. Her dad had helped this morning. She wasn't exactly sure how to put it in.

"I can help," Emily said, leaning in the doorway. "Daddy showed me earlier this week. I know how."

It grated on Cassie's nerves to accept Emily's help, but she nodded. "Okay."

Emily showed her how to moisten it and fit it in the holder. She gave her some more instructions, but Cassie shrugged her off. "I can take it from here."

She spent the next hour practicing blowing, making sure the sound coming out was on pitch. Then she pulled out the little lesson book inside the case. Following the finger drawings, she began playing notes. Even to her ears they sounded awkward and off-key, but she kept going.

When her dad got home an hour later, she was still practicing.

"Hey, that sounds good," he said, loosening his tie and dropping his briefcase by the piano. "Do you need help?"

"No." She smiled under his praise, then touched her lips, trying to bring some feeling back into them. Her whole mouth ached from the constant playing. "This is going to

take some work."

"But we did great for our first day." He picked his briefcase back up. "Keep practicing."

Cassie did, determined to be prepared for next Friday. She gave it several hours on Saturday, then one hour on Monday after school. By the time she got home from Girls' Club on Tuesday, she was too tired to give it a full hour, but she still gave it half an hour.

Wednesday she assembled the clarinet and then sat on the piano bench, staring at it. She just didn't feel it today.

"I've been practicing hard for days," Cassie told the piano. "I can take a break today." She put the clarinet down on the ground and went to her room.

She was laying on her bed reading when her dad knocked on the open door.

"Did you get your homework done?" he asked.

She rolled over. She could hear Emily on the piano in the dining room, the high notes pinging around Cassie's head and making her ears ring. A headache whispered at the corners of her brain, threatening to take over. "Yeah. Now I'm just reading."

"I saw your clarinet out by the piano."

"Oh. I forgot to put it away." She didn't move from the bed, though. Her eyes felt heavy, and she suddenly wanted to sleep.

"How long did you practice for?"

"I didn't." His image blurred in front of her, and Cassie took her glasses off to make sure they weren't dirty. "I'm pretty tired today."

"You won't improve if you don't practice, Cassie. You can't afford to take a break."

Cassie pressed a hand to her face and lay back on the bed. "I'm just really tired."

Her dad left the doorway. Cassie closed her eyes and went to sleep.

♥

She woke up in the morning with her head swimming. Her eyes didn't want to open, but she heard Emily and Scott fighting in the bathroom. She yanked herself out of bed and stumbled to the bathroom.

"Guys, be quiet!" she snapped in a harsh whisper. "You'll wake Mom!" Her head throbbed and her neck ached. She grabbed a toothbrush and sat down on the floor to brush, too exhausted to stay on her feet. Scaredy padded in next to her and whimpered, his tail giving a little thump. She realized she hadn't taken him outside during the night. Cassie groaned.

"You're gonna miss the bus," Emily said, pulling her light brown hair into a ponytail.

"What time is it? My alarm didn't go off!" Cassie hauled herself to her feet. She grabbed the sink and held herself there as a wave of dizziness washed over her.

"Yes, it did," Emily said. "You just didn't get up." She walked out of the bathroom.

"And you didn't wake me?" Cassie called after her. She ran to her room and threw on a t-shirt, then yanked on a pair of jeans. Her mom would have to take care of Scaredy.

The front door opened and closed, and Cassie forced

herself to move faster. If she missed the bus, she'd be in so much trouble. She grabbed her backpack from the foot of the bed and rushed out the door.

The cold air hit her like a million sharp needles, piercing her skin and cutting through her jacket. Cassie barely had a chance to register the temperature because she saw the bus already pulling up to the top of the hill. Sweat beaded on her forehead. She wasn't going to make it. Her side was already cramping.

"Wait for me!" she gasped out.

"Come on, come on," Kathy, the bus driver, said as Cassie stumbled to the open door.

She climbed on and collapsed in the first empty seat, which happened to be next to Emily. Cassie leaned her head against the seat and groaned.

"I made her hold the bus for you," Emily said. "I told her you were coming."

Cassie's eyes did not want to open. She squinted at Emily. "Thanks." She closed her eyes again. The bus jerked to a stop, and Cassie's eyes popped open. "What happened?"

"We're here." Emily gave her a sympathetic look. "You slept the whole way."

"Oh." She widened her eyes, trying to make them stop burning. She slipped her arm through her backpack and followed Emily off the bus.

♥

"How long have you been itching this spot on your head, Cassie?"

"Hm?" Cassie looked at Ms. Dawson and stopped scratching her forehead. She stood in line with her class, waiting to leave the cafeteria after lunch. "Oh. I don't know. I wasn't really paying attention."

"Ms. Wade, come here, please." Ms. Dawson beckoned to one of the other fifth grade teachers.

"What is it?" Ms. Wade asked, coming over.

"Look at this." Ms. Dawson pushed back Cassie's hair. "That spot on her forehead. She keeps scratching it."

"Well." Ms. Wade frowned. Cassie felt like a goldfish, the way the two women stared at her head. "What do you think it is?"

"How are you feeling, Cassie?" Ms. Dawson asked.

"Horrible," Cassie admitted. "I'm really tired and have a headache."

"Do you think it's the chicken pox?" Ms. Wade murmured, looking sideways at Ms. Dawson.

"I don't know. It's been so long since I've seen it." They both frowned at Cassie.

Cassie digested their words without comment. She'd heard of the chicken pox. Her mom had it when she was a girl, but Cassie had been vaccinated as a kid. She was pretty sure that meant she would never get the disease.

Ms. Dawson pressed the back of her hand against Cassie's forehead. "She doesn't feel feverish."

"Well, I guess we'll find out soon." Ms. Wade gave Cassie one last glance and returned to her class.

"Let me know if you start to feel sick, all right?"

Cassie nodded. She already felt sick, and she was pretty

sure she'd said that, but maybe she needed to feel sicker.

She spent the rest of the day trying to keep her head up. Her eyelids drooped every time she started reading, and her head nodded while she tried to write out her answers. She couldn't focus on anything Ms. Dawson said, and she spent recess sitting on the sidewalk, bundled in her winter coat and her arms wrapped around herself.

Finally the bell rang signaling the end of school. Cassie moved as fast as she could from the classroom to the bus circle just so she could get on the bus first. She picked a seat by the window and leaned her head against it. Her vision blurred, and Cassie closed her eyes.

♥

"Are you okay, Cassie?" her mom asked as Cassie dragged her feet in the door.

"No," she replied, too tired to mince words. "I'm going to bed." She dropped her backpack by the piano and went down the hall, not waiting for an answer. The pillow called her name. Her stomach tumbled over on itself, churning and grumbling. She wrapped her arms around her torso and curled up.

Cassie woke up, a bit groggy, her throat aching. She wasn't sure how long she'd slept. Her eyes slitted open. The weak light filtering through the blinds gave away that the day was ending, with night fast encroaching. Cassie sat up, her head heavy like it was full of cotton.

This end of the house was silent. She slipped out of bed and followed the murmur of voices to the kitchen. She wasn't hungry, though, so she sat down on the living room couch and watched her family eat.

Her mom noticed her first. "Hi, Cassie. Are you feeling any better?"

Cassie shrugged. "I think so." As long as she was sitting down, anyway, she didn't feel too bad. She lay down on the couch and rested her head on the armrest. She had an itch on her foot but was too tired to bend down and scratch it. She wiggled her toes, twisting her foot around to relieve the sensation.

If anything, the need only increased. Like a bunch of little ants walking in circles on the sole of her foot. And now they were tickling her with their little jaws.

Cassie grabbed her toes and tilted her foot so she could see the bottom. No little ants. She did notice, however, a tiny drop of water. She touched it with her finger and pulled her foot away. It wasn't water, but a small blister, and the moment she'd touched it, the itching had doubled. Now more than anything she just wanted to dig her fingers into that little blister and scratch it off. The first vestiges of panic crept up her chest. What was that? Leftovers from an ant attack? The beginnings of leprosy?

"Mom!" she called. "There's something weird on my foot!"

Her mom looked over from the table and frowned. "What is it?"

"I don't know." Cassie swallowed, trying to keep her voice calm. "Come see."

Her mom put her fork down, and the whole family stared as she made her way to Cassie. "It's all right, sweetie.

What's on your foot?"

Cassie twisted her foot around so the bottom of it faced her mom. Then she held her breath as her mom's fingers traced the outlines of the tiny blister. It tickled and itched painfully, all at the same time. Then her mom's finger trailed down her foot and paused near the heel. The same sensation occurred, thought slightly less sensitive now.

"What are you doing?" Cassie pushed herself up so she could watch.

"You didn't notice this one, did you?"

"There are two?" Her heart skipped a beat.

"It's the chicken pox, Cassie. I'm pretty sure you've got the chicken pox."

CHAPTER TWENTY-FOUR

Itchy

Cassie sat in a folding chair behind her dad, watching him pull up information on the internet. "But I thought the chicken pox was extinct," she said.

"There's a vaccine," he said. He had taken Cassie downstairs and set up a temporary room for her, away from the other kids. "You got it, and so did you brother and sisters. But it doesn't always work. Hopefully you'll only have a mild case because of that."

"And the others, will they get sick?"

"Maybe." He pulled up several pictures of people's faces covered in red sores, swollen lips, bruised ears.

"Ew!" Cassie recoiled. "Is that going to happen to me?"

He chuckled. "No. This is what used to happen in some extreme cases. Most people never got it this bad, even before the vaccine. You probably won't have more than a couple of poxes." He clicked on a few less dramatic images.

Cassie relaxed. The new images didn't look so bad. "Do I

have to miss school?" She made it sound like she'd be disappointed, but inside she envisioned a long vacation.

"I'm afraid so. You could still infect the kids that didn't get vaccinated. Even the ones that did might get it."

"Okay." She kept her eyes lowered to conceal her glee. It didn't look like she'd get very sick, and she had to stay home to keep from infecting anyone else. A win-win situation.

"You should rest now," her father told her. "Give your body a chance to fight this disease."

"Sure." Cassie stood up and bundled herself into the big blanket her mom had laid out on the cot. She curled up and closed her eyes, smiling as she imagined telling Riley. She doubted Riley had ever had the chicken pox.

❤

Cassie's mouth ached. Somewhere her body knew it was morning time, even though the basement room was dark, and the blankets covered her head. But she could barely move. Her tongue probed around her inner cheeks.

No, it didn't just ache; it itched. She rubbed her cheeks with her tongue, trying to relieve the sensation. When that didn't work, she reached a hand up and pushed her cheek against her teeth.

But that only brought to her attention that her hand itched. Cassie threw the blankets off her face and examined her arms. The same small white blisters dotted her exposed skin. She reached into the blankets and grabbed her foot. Flipping it over, Cassie searched for the little blisters. They were gone; in their places were round red sores. Just staring at them made her want to dig her fingers in and scratch.

She sucked in a breath, noting how her lips itched. Were these things on her face? Her fingers danced over her jaw and forehead, but all it did was increase the itching sensation.

She slung her legs over the side of the cot. Using the wall for support, Cassie made her way to the bathroom. The bright light assaulted her eyes, and she blinked several times before they adjusted and she could see.

There were three poxes on her face. She breathed a sigh of relief. It could definitely be worse. Her stomach tightened, and she leaned her head against the bathroom door. Standing took too much effort. She bent her knees and sat on the floor, wrapping her arms around her lower torso.

She didn't feel so good.

"Mom," she whispered. Clearing her throat, she tried again. "Mom! Mom!" She really put effort into the last yell, trying to force the sound past her lips and up the stairs. She must've succeeded, because she heard the thumping of footsteps above her. Then they were on the stairs, and finally they reached the basement.

"Cassie?"

"Mom." Cassie lifted her head enough to catch her mom's attention. Her mom came over and squatted beside her, pressing her hands around Cassie's face.

"How do you feel, honey?"

Cassie shook her head. She felt achy and sore. And her skin crawled like an invasion of invisible bugs.

"Let's get you back into bed." Her mom put an arm

around her and scooped her to her feet. "I'll bring you down some crackers and soup."

Cassie did not want crackers and soup. She closed her eyes, too tired to say anything more. Her mom lay her down on the cot and tucked the blankets around her.

"Would you like me to put on a movie for you? Your dad set up a TV in here."

Cassie lifted her eyes enough to see the small television resting on the folding chair, right in front of the cot. It was a thoughtful gesture on her dad's part, and it warmed Cassie's heart. But she couldn't keep her eyes open. They felt like lead, and they wanted to close. She meant to answer her mom, but sleep beckoned her.

♥

Her mom moved her daily projects downstairs and stayed close to Cassie. Annette came down a few times, but each time Mrs. Jones shooed her back upstairs. Cassie would wake up long enough to stare out at her mom through half-closed eyes, but then she'd drift back off just as quickly.

And then one time, she didn't. "Mom. Mom!"

"I'm here, Cassie." Mrs. Jones crouched next to the cot.

"I'm hungry," Cassie said, chewing on the itchiness in her cheeks.

"I'll warm up your soup and bring it right down."

That soup sounded wonderful now. Cassie pushed herself into a sitting position in anticipation. Her hands wandered to her legs, mindlessly scratching, then up to her neck, then her elbow.

"Don't scratch, Cassie," her mom said, coming in with a tray of soup and crackers.

"I'm not scratching," she said, and then realized she was. She placed her hands on the tray, concentrating on not thinking about the itch behind her ear. She took a spoonful of soup. Her palm itched and the spot behind her ear was spreading. The warm soup went down her throat and

tasted wonderfully soothing. But it did not take away the insane itch behind her ear, on her palm, or the new one behind her knee.

"I can't take the itching!" she cried.

"Finish your soup and you can take a bath in tea tree oil."

"What's that? Will it help?" Cassie scraped her hands up her legs and dug her nails into the skin behind her knees.

"It should."

"Did you get the chicken pox when you were little?"

Her mom paused, her brown eyes staring into space as she thought about the question. "Yes. Almost everyone did. There was no vaccination then."

"Did you get it bad?"

"I don't really remember. I was only four. I survived, at least."

Cassie finished up her soup, her whole mind intent on getting a bath that would relieve the itching. Her mom helped her get it ready, and then Cassie climbed inside. She shut her eyes in satisfaction. The warm water soothed her, and the itching stopped.

"I think it's working," she said.

"Good. Take your time, and let me know when you're ready to get out."

The bath was relaxing and comfortable, but after a few minutes, Cassie got bored. She called her mom to help her get out.

"Is the itching better?" Mrs. Jones asked, pulling Cassie's long hair back into a French braid.

Cassie rubbed the cloth of her shirt against an itch. "It was better in the bath. But it's horrible again!" The itching was going to drive her crazy. Tears stung her eyes, and she sniffed.

"Just think about other things, honey. Come on, let's put on a movie."

"Is there a movie you want to watch?" Mrs. Jones asked once Cassie was settled in her cot.

Cassie flipped through the TV Guide. "No, actually. Go to channel five. There's a show on TV I want to watch."

The television changed to the requested channel, but the static was so bad, Cassie could hardly make out the figures. She scowled. "Are the settings right?"

"Oh." Her mom left the room and then came back. "It's raining. We might not be getting very many channels right now."

"Great." Cassie's brain pounded inside her skull as if it were an animal trying to get out. "Put on any movie, then, I don't care." She closed her eyes and waited for the sound of a movie to reach her ears.

When she opened her eyes, she realized she'd fallen asleep again. A movie was playing, but Cassie guessed it to be about halfway over. There were still crackers on the tray next to her cot, and she picked them up and ate them.

Another bath would be nice. At least for a few moments she hadn't itched.

She thought about calling her mom again, but that required too much energy. Instead she watched the movie, waiting for someone to check on her.

The movie was almost over when she heard the front door slam open, followed by pounding upstairs. Annette's excited babble mixed with Scott's whiny tone and Emily's bossy one. Then one set of feet came down the stairs. Cassie listened to them approach, not sure if she should pretend to be asleep or greet them.

Emily came into the room, her light brown hair in disarray around her flushed face, the plush jacket still on and zipped nearly to her chin. "Here," she said, tossing a bunch of papers at Cassie.

Cassie caught one as they fluttered to the ground. "What are these?"

"Your homework." Emily grinned at her. "Mom told me to tell the office you're sick. They gave me that for you."

Cassie glared at her. Could this sickness get any worse? Now on top of not feeling well, she had to do homework! "I'd go to school if I could, you know."

"Yep. And hopefully you'll be able to soon!" Emily started to leave, and then she put her hand on the door jam and turned around. "Oh, and did you forget tomorrow's band practice? Looks like you'll be too sick."

Jerk! Cassie thought, shooting daggers with her eyes into her sister's retreating back. All that relentless practicing she'd done every day until she got sick, and now no one would even know. To make it worse, she might have even forgotten everything. It would still be Emily, the queen of music, the queen of everything.

❤

Cassie's mom gave her another bath that evening, this time with baking soda. It didn't seem to help anymore than the tea tree oil one. She sat on the couch during dinner and cried, feeling miserable and lonely.

Mrs. Jones came to the couch and handed the phone to her. "It's Riley. I called her for you."

Sniffing, Cassie pressed the phone to her ear. They hadn't talked since Wednesday. "Hello?"

"Hi," Riley's voice came back. "Your mom said you're

sick."

"Yeah." Tears welled up in her eyes and rolled down her cheeks. "I have the chicken pox."

"Ms. Dawson told us. Are you okay?"

"I feel horrible." Cassie tried to control the quaver in her voice, but she couldn't.

"I hope you feel better soon."

"Thanks."

Silence reigned on the phone, and Riley said, "Well, I better go."

"Yeah." Cassie nodded. "See you later." She put the phone down beside her, not feeling any better at all.

"We'll miss you at band practice tomorrow," Mr. Jones said as he tucked Cassie into her cot. He wrapped the blankets around her and smoothed back her hair. "You look like you have pepperoni all over your face."

"Thanks a lot, Daddy," Cassie said, but she knew he was teasing, and she didn't mind it. Her dad was often so stressed out from work that he wasn't funny.

Something seemed to be going on upstairs. Cassie heard footsteps thumping hard down the hall, followed by muffled crying.

"Jim?" Mrs. Jones called. "I need you to come up here."

"Better see what's wrong." He stood up, brushing his hands on his pants.

"Should I come see what's wrong?" Cassie asked, worried.

"No, stay here. Good night." He turned the light off in her room and walked out. Cassie tuned her ears in, trying to make sense of the scattered noises she heard.

Emily was crying. She shut herself in the room and the sound disappeared, but Cassie was too curious. She waited a moment longer to see if anyone would say anything, but everyone seemed to have gone to bed. The house was quiet. Cassie put her feet on the carpet and crept up the stairs, using the banister for support.

The light was still on in her parents' room. She followed it down the hall, slowing when she heard their murmur of voices. She couldn't make out what they said, though. From here she could hear the quiet sobs coming from her and Emily's room. Cassie peeked around the corner and saw her mom at the dresser, putting something away. She cleared her throat and tapped on the open door. Her mom looked up, and her dad poked his head out of the closet.

"Sorry," she said, doing her best to look concerned and not nosy, "I heard Emily crying. Is she okay?"

"She'll be fine," her mom said with a heavy sigh. "She's got the chicken pox."

CHAPTER TWENTY-FIVE
Band Practice

"Sorry that you have to miss band practice too," Cassie said. She was back in her room now, since Emily was sick also. Her dad had taken down the bunk bed so neither girl would have to exert herself, and now they both had a twin bed next to each other. "I know how much you were looking forward to it."

Emily nodded in response but didn't say anything else. The poxes covered most of her face, and even her lips looked swollen. A single tear shimmered on her lower lashes.

Cassie felt bad for her. She was into day three of being sick and day two of being home, and today seemed better than yesterday. Emily was only on day one, though. She still had two more days before she started to feel better.

"Look at it this way," Cassie said, her voice full of fake cheer. "Scott's not going to get our homework for us, so at least it will be a relaxing weekend."

Emily sort-of smiled. Her hands came up, and she raked them down her face.

"Don't do that." Cassie grabbed her hands and pulled them down. "It just gets worse. I promise. Try not to touch it." She settled back onto her bed and tried to think what she and Emily could do for fun. "Want to play Uno?"

Emily didn't answer, and Cassie swung her head around to look at her. Her eyes were closed, her chest rising in falling in sleep. Cassie snuggled deeper into her own blankets, her body echoing the primitive urge to take a nap.

♥

"Hello, Wildcats! It's a freezing Friday morning, isn't it?" Mr. Jones grinned across the music room at the handful of students who had arrived early for band practice. "Not too much longer, and we'll see sunshine and flowers."

Most of the kids just stared back at him with deadpan expressions, but Cassie grinned back. Her dad loved doing this band thing.

"And I'm very happy to have my daughters back today!" he said, pointing his baton at Cassie and Emily. "Both of them decided to prove that vaccinations don't work. Now that they've made their point, they're here, bright and early."

Cassie and Emily exchanged a smile. Cassie straightened in her chair, holding her clarinet at the ready. She'd been practicing. She felt more confident now, certain she could play whatever note he told them to.

"All right, everyone, instruments up. Once again, give me

a Middle C!"

The interesting panel of musical notes filled the room, though this time, even to Cassie's untrained ears, it sounded more in tune. Her dad walked around, listening, complimenting, correcting. He stopped at Emily first and congratulated her on her posture and the way she carried the note. Then he reached Cassie.

"Beautiful, Cassie," he said, making the "okay" symbol with his hand. "Great job."

Cassie didn't stop blowing her note, but inside she beamed.

♥

"How's your band practice going?" Leigh Ann asked Cassie as the girls gathered after school on Tuesday for their weekly Girls' Club meeting.

"It's great!" Cassie said. She sat down at one of the lunch tables left out for them to use. "We're learning a song to play for the school in an assembly. I play the clarinet!"

"I've always wanted to play an instrument," Leigh Ann said wistfully. She twisted a strand of curly brown hair around her finger. "Maybe someday."

"You could always join us," Cassie suggested. "We could use more people."

Riley came over and sat down next to her. "I don't like musical instruments. I think they're boring."

"Well, that's your opinion," Leigh Ann said, bolder than Cassie would ever dare to be. She wished she could say something like that.

Trisha, the assistant Girls' Club leader, walked in with a

big cardboard box in her arms. Margaret, Maureen's mom and the leader, came in behind her.

"Small group today, huh?" Margaret said, putting her arm around Maureen and hugging her.

Cassie glanced around. Her, Leigh Ann, Riley, and Cheyenne. Half of their normal size. "Where are Stacy and Janice? Jaiden?" She chanced to meet Trisha's eyes for a second and then looked away. She and Trisha had had an altercation at the beginning of the school year, and though they never spoke of it now, Cassie didn't have any warm and fuzzy feelings toward her. But she was Jaiden's mom, so she should know where Jaiden was.

"Stacy's got the chicken pox," Trisha said, her stern gaze landing on Cassie. "Her mom came and got her after lunch. And I made Jaiden stay home just in case it was still going around."

Even though she didn't come out and accuse Cassie of anything, the accusation hung in the air. Cassie shrank down at the lunch table and resisted the urge to glance around. Hopefully no one else blamed her.

Margaret cast a concerned glance Cassie's way. "The important thing is that everyone's okay. Cassie's not sick anymore and Maureen will be fine. So let's get started on today's project, shall we?"

Cassie tried to put Trisha from her mind and pay attention as they learned how to make friendship bracelets, but the woman's negative aura hung over Cassie like a dark cloud, casting a shadow on everything she tried to do.

Riley waited until Trisha walked away, then she leaned

over and spoke in Cassie's ear. "Don't let her get to you. Just think about how many friends you have."

Cassie nodded. Good advice. The more she thought about it, it was great advice. She had friends. She had Leigh Ann, and Riley, and . . . Well, the rest were only so-so friends, including Danelle. Cassie frowned. She needed more. Maybe it was time to reach out a little more.

Episode 5: Miss Popular

CHAPTER TWENTY-SIX
Birthday Plans

"It's March!" Cassie burst through the front door of her house and tossed her jacket at the hall closet. Scott and Emily paraded in behind her. They'd just gotten off the bus after a long day at school.

She'd known yesterday, of course, that today would be the first day of March. But sitting in class all day writing down the date on every piece of paper just made her giddy and excited. "Mom!"

She wandered into the kitchen, but her mom wasn't there. Scott and Emily began searching for snacks, but Cassie continued through the house. No one in the laundry room. She went down the stairs, one hand on the banister as she skidded over the carpet. "Mom! Mom!"

"In here," her mother finally called back.

Cassie rounded the corner to her mom's office. She had the sewing machine out and several pieces of fabric spread out on the floor. "What are you making?" Cassie asked, momentarily distracted.

"New placemats," her mom said. "I think we could use an update."

Cassie nodded and then turned back to the item on her mind. "So it's March!"

Her mom kept her eyes on the spool of thread as she placed it on her machine, but Cassie saw the smile that played at the corners of her mouth. "Yes, it is. Maybe it will finally start to get warm."

Warmth, spring, those were great things, but not what Cassie wanted to talk about. "And my birthday's in a week." She beamed at her mother.

"Oh, is it?" Finally Mrs. Jones turned to face her. Like Cassie, she wore glasses, though hers were brown frames while Cassie's were large and turquoise with colored dots embedded in them.

Cassie rolled her eyes, not falling for it. "Yes! I know you haven't forgotten. I'm going to be eleven!"

They didn't have a lot of friends over or do a big party for birthdays, but Mrs. Jones always made a beautiful cake. "Can we look through your cake books and pick one?" Cassie asked. It was her favorite part about birthdays.

"In a minute." Her mom picked up a few pieces of fabric and inserted pins around them. "Go get the cake books and start looking through them."

"Sure!" Cassie hopped back upstairs. She crouched in front of the cupboards and fingered the cake decorating books. She found one that looked newer than the others and pulled it out. The bright colors and varied cake shapes held her attention.

Her mom found her that way, sitting on the kitchen floor and sifting through the book. "Didn't want to use the table, Cassie?"

Cassie laughed and stood up, carrying the book with her. "I just got too involved. I think I found the one I want."

"Which is it?" Mrs. Jones sat down across from her, propping her chin up and looking at the pages.

"This one." Cassie pointed to a rectangular cake decorated like a dollar bill in white and green frosting. But instead of a picture of a famous political figure, it had the picture of a little boy cut out and placed in the middle. Cassie imagined her fifth-grade picture in the middle of the cake, as if she were someone important and famous. "Can you do it?"

Her mom pulled the book toward her and examined it. "Sure. This doesn't look too hard. But remember, Cassie, you can only have two friends over."

"I know." Cassie rubbed her hands together, unable to contain the excitement she felt. "I'll ask them tomorrow."

♥

A few months ago, the choice of who to invite would have been easy. Riley and Danelle were Cassie's best friends. But lately, Cassie didn't feel as close to Danelle. She couldn't pinpoint anything in particular that had happened. They just didn't hang out as much.

On the other hand, she and Riley had become closer. Cassie had spent the night at her house a few times, and they saw each other every Tuesday at Girls' Club. They didn't always get along, and sometimes Riley seemed mad at her for no reason. But Cassie knew for sure she'd invite her.

Riley brought it up before Cassie did. She sat next to her at lunch. "You're birthday's this Saturday, right?"

"Right," Cassie said, unable to keep the smile from her face.

"Are you having a party?"

"Yes! A slumber party on Friday night. You're coming, right?"

"Of course!" Riley grinned back at her. "Sounds great! Who else is coming?"

"Well, I haven't invited anyone else yet. But probably Danelle."

Riley took a bite of her carrot and nodded. "I could have guessed. Who else?"

Cassie hesitated. "Well, if Danelle can come, no one. If she can't, I'll have to invite someone else."

Now Riley frowned. "What do you mean? You won't invite anyone else?"

She sounded so annoyed that Cassie felt embarrassed. "No. I'm only allowed to have two people over."

"Just two people?" Riley echoed. "That's not much of a party."

"It is if it's my best friends," Cassie said, defensive.

Riley shrugged. "Yeah. I guess." She ate another carrot strip and didn't ask anymore questions.

Danelle wasn't sitting by Cassie at lunch, and some of the wind had gone out of Cassie's sails. Still, she tracked her down at recess. Danelle didn't like to swing anymore; instead she spent her time batting at the tether ball with another group of kids.

"Hi, Danelle," Cassie said as she approached.

"Hi, Cassie," Danelle said, glancing over briefly before slugging away at the ball again. It seemed like a pointless game to Cassie, hitting the ball just so the cord could wrap around the pole. Maybe there was something to it that she didn't understand. "Can I talk to you for a sec?"

"Sure," Danelle said, dropping her arms and backing away from the group. She led Cassie to the grass and turned to face her.

"What's up?" she asked, crossing her arms over her chest. Danelle was a bigger girl than Riley and already had the beginnings of a woman's chest, something that Cassie couldn't help envying.

"My birthday's this Saturday," she said, exhaling the words. "I'm having a slumber party Friday night. Want to come?"

Danelle smiled, flashing her metallic braces. "Oh. I don't know. I'll talk to my dad."

"Sure."

"Thanks for asking." Danelle gave her a wave as she rejoined her tetherball friends. "See you around!"

♥

Cassie crouched beside Riley's desk before school started in the morning. "So did you ask your mom about my party?" she asked, breathless from having run all the way from the bus loop.

"Yeah, she said it's fine," Riley said, doodling a pretty girl with a heart-shaped face and big hips on her paper. "But she'll be out of town, so my dad will bring me over."

"Are you having a party this weekend?" Mikaela Reese, the girl who sat next to Riley, asked. "Oo, fun! Why?"

Cassie's cheeks burned, embarrassed to have been overheard. "It's my birthday Saturday."

Mikaela's eyes widened. "Really? How amazing! It's mine too!"

"Oh, yeah?" Cassie had never met someone before with her same birthday. "Will you be eleven, too?"

"Yep!" Mikaela grinned at her. Then she frowned. "I haven't decided when to do my party. I might do it Saturday. Or Friday." She looked at Cassie. "Would that be bad, if my party were the same day as yours?"

Riley frowned at Mikaela. "Yeah, I can't go to yours if you do it the same day as Cassie."

Mikaela nodded. "Okay. I'll plan a slumber party for Saturday, then. You're invited too, Cassie."

"Thanks," Cassie said, not bothering to explain that she wouldn't be there. Her family had strict rules about honoring the Sabbath, and one of them was no birthday parties on a Sunday. She moved to Danelle's desk next.

"Did you find out if you can come on Friday?"

"Yeah, I don't know yet," Danelle said, tapping her pencil from the eraser to the point and back again on her desk. "But I'll find out, okay?"

"Okay," Cassie said, feeling foolish for asking.

The final bell rang, and Ms. Dawson hit the bell on her

desk. Cassie backed away from Danelle and sat down to begin her morning exercises.

The next day when Cassie walked into class, she found a white envelope on her desk. Glancing around, Cassie saw that every girl's desk in the classroom also had one. Some students were already opening theirs.

Excited, Cassie slid the card out from inside. An invitation.

Come celebrate! You're invited to Mikaela Reese's 11th birthday party!

Cassie flipped it open and read the inside.

This Friday at 4pm, bring your pillow and pajamas over for a slumber party!

An address followed, but Cassie put the invitation aside. A hard rock formed in the pit of her stomach. She'd already known she wouldn't be going to Mikaela's party. But now she'd gone and planned to have it on the same day as Cassie's.

♥

"So I got an invite to Mikaela's party," Cassie said at lunch. She'd opted for salad bar today also, and she followed behind Riley, adding ham squares and sliced fruit to her tray.

"Really? Even though she knows your party is the same night? That's weird." Riley threw on a bunch of bell peppers, and Cassie made a face. She didn't know how her friend could to eat those; Cassie couldn't even stand the smell.

"I guess she was just trying to be nice."

"Or maybe she wants you to skip your party and come to hers. Hey." Riley blinked her greenish-brown eyes at Cassie. "That's not a bad idea. You could do a double birthday party."

Cassie shook her head. They walked to the next open spot and sat down at the table. "No. My mom is already making my cake. It's going to be amazing."

"Well, it's still a good idea." Riley opened her milk and took a sip.

Cassie's grip tightened on her fork as a sudden fear hit her. "You're not going to go to Mikaela's party, are you?"

"And ditch my best friend?" Riley frowned at her over the milk carton. "You should know better."

Cassie's shoulders relaxed, and she nodded. "Of course." She'd just had to make sure.

CHAPTER TWENTY-SEVEN
Pregnant Cat

"This is the cake you want?" Mrs. Jones asked Cassie after dinner. She had her cake book out, along with a pad of paper.

Cassie came and leaned against her mom's back, looking over her shoulder. "Yes!"

Her mom began making a list of the supplies she would need. "What picture do you want in the middle?"

"My fifth-grade class picture," Cassie said without hesitation. She'd already considered other photos, but that one was the best. Her mom had curled her long brown hair, and she wore a pretty red dress. Cassie thought it was one of the best pictures of her.

"Perfect. Bring me one, and I'll start working on the cake tomorrow."

Cassie skipped to her room. She pulled out the photo album she kept under her bed and found one of her school pictures. Then she returned to the kitchen. "Here you go!"

Her mother paperclipped it to the list. "Which friends are coming?"

Cassie ticked them off on her fingers. "Riley is for sure. Danelle still doesn't know."

"When is Danelle going to give you an answer?"

She shrugged. "I'll ask her again tomorrow."

Her mom added a few more things to her list. "And what flavor cake do you want?"

"Strawberry. And strawberry ice-cream." She rubbed her hands together in anticipation.

"Mom?" Scott came into the kitchen. He still wore his heavy jacket, and his face was flushed as if he'd been outside. "Something's wrong with Baby Blue."

Baby Blue was their beautiful Siamese cat. Their dad got her and Pioneer, a dog, when the family moved into the new house . "Is she up in a tree?" Cassie asked. Usually if there were a problem, that was it. The cat knew how to get up trees, but she was clueless about getting down.

"No. She's just sitting in the grass and won't get up. She meows at me but won't come close." His forehead wrinkled in concern, and for a moment he looked thirty instead of six. "I think she's hurt."

"Well, let's go see." Mrs. Jones abandoned the cake book and followed Scott outside. Cassie came too, more out of curiosity than worry for the cat.

Annette and Emily were playing in the yard. They ran over and joined the group.

"What's going on?" Emily asked.

"Something's wrong with Baby Blue," Cassie answered.

Already her mind was back in the kitchen, wanting to finish planning her birthday party.

"Oh, no!" Annette cried, her little eyes widening.

"I'm sure she's fine," Cassie said. "Don't worry about her."

She sat on a bunch of twigs and leaves. She looked up at them as they approached and meowed.

"What's wrong, Baby?" Mrs. Jones murmured, running her hand along the cat's spine. She purred and lifted her rump, but didn't get up. Mrs. Jones put her hands under her belly and gently picked her up.

"Ah," she said with a smile, "I see what's wrong."

"What is it?" Scott leaned closer, brows all pinched together. "Is she okay?"

"She's pregnant." Mrs. Jones cuddled the cat to her chest.

"Pregnant!" Cassie gasped out.

"So she's going to have babies?" Scott asked uncertainly.

"Puppies!" Annette exclaimed, clapping her hands.

"Kittens," Cassie said. She wanted to clap her hands with her younger sister. How fun that would be! Little tiny cats running around.

"We need to make a private place for her in the house." Mrs. Jones walked back around to the front door. "I don't want her having kittens out here."

❤

Cassie could hardly wait to tell Riley her cat was pregnant. Maybe she'd have the kittens before the party. What fun that would be! She walked into the classroom and set her backpack down. She turned around and frowned.

All the girls were crowded around Mikaela's desk, giggling and laughing.

"My dad's renting the movies," Mikaela said in a conspiratorial whisper. "And my brother might bring his friends over!"

That brought another peel of giggles. Cassie's heart sank. Both Danelle and Riley were in the midst of Mikaela's groupies.

Mikaela spotted her. "Cassie!" She beckoned her over. "You know, I think you having your birthday party the same day isn't a good idea. Why don't you cancel yours and just come to mine? It's going to be awesome."

"That was my suggestion, too," Riley said.

Cassie shook her head, willing herself not to cry. "That's okay. I want to have my own party. And Riley said she's coming." She looked at Riley, waiting for her to back her up.

"But Riley wants to come to my party," Mikaela said. "It's not fair for you to put her in that position."

"But she's my best friend," Cassie said.

"Well, I have lots of best friends," Riley said. "Mikaela's one of them."

"Yeah." Mikaela slung an arm around Riley's shoulder and grinned.

"But Riley, you said you'd come to my party," Cassie said, hating that they were having this conversation in the classroom, in front of everyone.

"Yeah, yeah, okay," Riley snapped, crossing her arms over her chest. "I haven't forgotten."

Cassie looked at Danelle, not expecting a positive response. "Are you coming?"

"Uh . . ." Danelle toyed with her earlobe. "I still don't know. I'll have to call you."

Cassie nodded and went to her desk without another word. She pulled out her notebook for morning exercises and began the work, holding her pencil tightly to stifle the trembling. She took several deep breaths. She couldn't cry. Not here. She couldn't let them think it was a big deal.

CHAPTER TWENTY-EIGHT

Invitations

Cassie didn't have time to fret over her friends once she got home, though.

"She's in labor," her mom said. She pulled Cassie over to the couch. Baby Blue had secured herself behind it. Annette was already crouched there, staring into the crevice between the couch and the wall.

"Your sister's been there for an hour," Mrs. Jones whispered, giving Cassie a conspiratorial smile. "Your cake's in the oven. Help me get it out. Annette will tell us if anything changes with the cat."

"Okay," Cassie said, her mind returning to her impending party.

She helped her mom remove the cake from the oven, closing her eyes to breathe in the warm strawberry aroma.

"So who's coming?" Mrs. Jones asked. She set the cake on the counter. Cassie knew it would cool over night, and tomorrow her mom would ice it. Just in time for the party.

If there was a party.

She pushed the thought away, but the dark heaviness in her chest remained. "Just Riley, I think. Danelle never gives me an answer."

Her mom tsked and gave her a sideways glance. "You think? Hasn't Riley said yes?"

"Yeah, she did, but. . . ." Cassie's voice trailed off. Then she shook herself. Riley wouldn't let her down. "Yeah, she's coming."

Mrs. Jones narrowed her eyes. "What's going on?"

Cassie didn't want to admit this to her mom. It made it sound as if everyone liked Mikaela more than her. Maybe they did. "Well, Mikaela's having a party tomorrow night. She invited Riley. I think Riley wants to go."

Her mom folded her arms and pursed her lips. "But Riley knows you can only have two people, right? And that she's one of them?"

"Yeah, yeah, she knows." Cassie played with the edge of a fraying rag. "She'll come."

"One person, then." Her mom shrugged. "It'll be fun. We'll rent a movie and get some pizza."

Cassie smiled back, but she knew it was weak. Every time she thought about her party, her stomach twisted in knots. And not the excited kind.

Annette let out a shriek from the living room. "You guys! There's a kitten!"

Cassie ran back to the couch, her mom right behind her. Emily and Scott also ran over.

Baby Blue licked the small black bundle huddled beneath

her. The tiny thing threw its head back and let out a little mew.

"Oh!" Cassie said. "It's so cute!"

"Give her space," Mrs. Jones said, pulling the children back. "There are more kittens in there. This is a private moment for cats."

Cassie went into the dining room and put together her clarinet. She practiced for a minute, and then went back to check on the cat. Still just one black kitten, his face tucked into Baby Blue's belly. Cassie returned to her clarinet.

A little while later, Emily came in. "Where's Mom?"

"I don't know. I'm practicing."

"How long does it take for the other kittens to get here? There's still only one."

"I'm sure she's fine," Cassie said. But she wasn't sure. She put down her clarinet and wandered with Emily down the hall to her parents' room.

"Mom?" Emily said. "Shouldn't there be more kittens by now?"

Her mom frowned over the towels she folded on her bed. "There's still only one?"

Cassie nodded. "Yeah."

Mrs. Jones went back to the living room, and the girls followed. They stared behind the couch at Baby Blue for a long while before Mrs. Jones straightened.

"I better make sure everything's all right. Cassie, help your dad get dinner ready and don't wait up for me. We might be late."

Cassie heard the undercurrent of tension in her mother's voice. "Is something wrong with Baby Blue?"

"Get me a box for the cat and her kitten. I'll take them both to the doctor."

Cassie blinked back tears as she got a cardboard box and lined it with a towel. It seemed wrong somehow to be packing up Baby Blue and her brand new baby. This should be a happy moment. The two cats belonged here, at their house. Not in the sterile clinic of a vet somewhere.

"What's going to happen to her?" Emily asked, coming to help pack down the towel.

"Nothing. They might have to do a C-section to get the kittens out." Cassie kept her voice calm. No reason to freak Emily out, also.

"What's a C-section?"

"Where they cut you open to get your baby."

"What?" Emily gasped. She wrapped her arms around her navel. "But that will kill her!"

"No, silly. It's very safe. She'll be fine." At least, Cassie hoped so. She crossed her mental fingers.

CHAPTER TWENTY-NINE
Taking Sides

Danelle never did call, but Cassie hadn't expected her to. By the time she got to school on Friday, she pretty much knew Danelle wasn't coming. She didn't know what to worry about more: her party that night, or her mom with the cat. There hadn't been any time in the morning to track down her mom and see how they were.

She must've been wearing her heart on her sleeve, because Ms. Dawson asked, "Is everything all right, Cassie?"

She hesitated. "I'm fine. Just worried about my cat." No need to bring up the party. "She was supposed to have kittens last night but only had one. So my mom took her to the vet."

"Oh, no. Well, these things work out, Cassie. Let me know how it goes."

Cassie supposed that advice applied to everything in life. "I will."

Riley didn't sit by Cassie at lunch, so Cassie sat next to Andrea.

"Where's Riley?" Andrea asked. She exchanged bags of chips with Kristin, the girl on the other side of her.

Cassie shrugged. "Hanging out with her new best friend, I guess."

Andrea quirked up an eyebrow. "Mikaela?"

"Yeah."

"Don't worry, it will pass," Kristin said. "She thinks Mikaela's all cool now because of the big party."

"But I'm having a party tonight, too," Cassie said, her frustration coloring her words. "And Riley said she'd be there. She promised! Now she talks like she's about to ditch me for Mikaela's stupid party."

"Really?" Andrea's eyebrows shot up. "No way. We'd never ditch a friend like that." She looked at Kristin for affirmation.

"Right." Kristin nodded her head. "Friends don't do that to each other."

"Well." Cassie sighed and opened her milk carton. "I hope Riley knows that."

"I'd come to your party instead of Mikaela's," Andrea said. "It sounds lame to me. I'm not going."

Cassie gave her a small smile. "Looks like I invited the wrong people."

♥

"You're not coming, are you?" Cassie stopped Danelle at recess before she ran off to the tether balls.

"Yeah, I can't come," Danelle said, wrinkling her nose

and frowning. "I'm sorry."

Cassie felt a flash of anger. For how long had Danelle known she wasn't coming? Why hadn't she just said so? Even worse, was she going to Mikaela's party?

But in the end, none of that mattered, so Cassie shoved the thoughts from her mind. "Sure, it's fine." She turned and walked toward the swings, and she knew then that her friendship with Danelle was over. She was glad that Danelle wasn't coming. They wouldn't have had fun together.

Riley didn't join Cassie at the swings. Cassie swung by herself, wondering if she'd be having a party by herself, also.

♥

Cassie didn't get the chance to talk to Riley until they were walking out to the bus. "You're coming tonight, right?"

Riley hesitated. "Everyone's going to be at Mikaela's party. It will be so fun. You should come."

Cassie forced a laugh. "I'm not missing my own birthday."

"But it's not really a party. You're just having some people over."

"With a cake and ice-cream, and pizza, and a movie," Cassie said stiffly, her lips not wanting to move. "It's a party."

Riley shrugged. "Okay."

"Okay, you'll be there?" Cassie asked.

"I said I would, right?" Riley glared up at the sun and got

on her bus.

Some of the weight lifted off Cassie's chest. At least she'd have Riley.

"Hey," Betsy said, greeting Cassie as she climbed on the bus. "Are you okay? You look upset."

She sighed. Was she so easy to read? "Tomorrow's my birthday."

"Happy birthday! Isn't that a happy thing?"

"Yeah, except . . . only one person's coming to my party."

Betsy's green eyes grew large in surprise. "What? Why?"

"Because I'm only allowed to have two people, and one of them told me today she can't come. So it's just the other one."

"Oh, Cassie." Betsy put an arm around Cassie's shoulders and hugged her close. "I'm so sorry."

Cassie seized Betsy's hand. "Betsy. I have an idea. You could come!"

"I'd love to come. You really want me to?"

"Yes!" Cassie leaned back in the seat, blinking back the sudden tears. Riley's less-than-stellar response and Danelle's attitude were finally getting to her. "You're my friend. It starts at five at my house."

"I'll ask my mom. I'll try my hardest, okay?"

"Yes." Cassie dug a piece of paper from her backpack. "Here's my phone number. Your mom can call my mom and she'll give you directions and work out all the details. It's a slumber party, so bring your stuff—"

Betsy put her hand on Cassie's paper. "We don't have a phone, so don't worry about that. And I know where you live."

Cassie pulled her glasses off and wiped her eyes. She nodded. "Okay. Okay."

♥

"There's the birthday girl!" Mrs. Jones greeted cheerfully as Cassie walked in, Scaredy at her heels. Her mom frowned when she saw her face. "What's wrong?"

"Nothing." Cassie shook her head, clearing off her emotions. She gave a tentative smile. "Everything's great. Can't wait for tonight."

"Look." Mrs. Jones put her hands on Cassie's shoulders and steered her into the kitchen. "Look at your cake." She beamed down at it.

It was the most beautiful cake Cassie had ever seen. Exactly like a dollar bill, only it had the number "11" in the corners. Right smack in the middle was Cassie's smiling fifth-grade photo. Cassie's heart surged with pride for her mother's work. "It's amazing." She turned around and hugged her. "I can't wait for my friends to see it." This was cool. The cake was fantastic.

"Your dad's bringing home the pizza. He'll stop and get a movie, too. Do you know what you want to watch?"

Cassie shook her head. "Just tell him not to get a dumb Western."

"Of course. Do you have homework? You better get it done before Riley gets here."

"Yeah." She turned to run off, then spun back around. "Oh yeah! Baby Blue! Is she okay? What happened?"

Her mother's expression changed, one eyebrow quirking

up and the corner of a lip curving. "She's fine." She went into the laundry room. Cassie followed her and found Baby Blue curled up in the same box, her belly completely shaved with a line of stitches up the center. Her black baby hung off one nipple, his little paws gripping her exposed flesh as he suckled.

"And the kittens?" Cassie asked, resisting the urge to pick up the cat and check underneath her.

Her mom shook her head. "There's still only one."

Cassie's eyes widened. "Did the others die?" she whispered, horrified.

"No. The vet felt around and agreed that there had to be more kittens in there. So, he cut her open." Her mom gestured at the shaved belly. "He felt around and said, 'oh yes, there's definitely one more. I can feel the kitten.' And then—" She shook her head. "It wasn't a kitten. She just had a full bladder."

"A full bladder?" Cassie echoed.

Her mom nodded and started to laugh. "Baby only had one kitten. Poor cat! We cut the poor thing open for no reason!"

"Was he sorry?" Cassie asked, astonished. How could a vet not know the difference between a bladder and a kitten?

"Oh, yes, he kept saying he was sorry. He was so embarrassed. He didn't even charge us for the operation."

"Well, I suppose that's good. And the kitten's fine?"

Mrs. Jones nodded. "The kitten's fine. Now go get your homework done before Riley gets here."

CHAPTER THIRTY
No Shows

Cassie ran off to her room. She worked on her school assignments until she heard her dad walk in the door.

"Daddy!" she cried, joining Annette, her youngest sister, in the welcoming committee.

"There's the birthday girl!" Mr. Jones said as she threw her arms around his waist. "Here, help bring these pizzas in."

"Wow, so many." Cassie took the box on top and carried it into the kitchen. "Four? Who's going to eat all this?"

"Well, isn't someone having a party?"

"I can eat it all," Scott said. He was doing Cassie's job at the dishwasher, and didn't look too happy about it.

"What time is Riley coming, Cassie?" her mom asked. She set out party plates on the table. "We're ready to start."

Cassie glanced at the digital clock on the oven, surprised to notice that it was already five o'clock. "I told her five. I'm sure she'll be here soon." She went to the counter and opened the plastic forks. Anything to distract herself from the time. "Did you get the ice-cream?"

"Strawberry. Just like you wanted."

Cassie rocked back and forth on her feet. "I'm going on the deck to play with Scaredy." With the warmer weather approaching, her dog had decided he'd rather be outside than in. Their walks together got longer and longer until Cassie gave up and just let him spend his time outside.

"Sure," her mom said. "If you see Riley's dad's truck coming up the road, come back in."

"I will."

Scaredy happily crawled into her lap, his tail thumping against her thigh. She petted his head, but her mind wasn't on her dog. Cassie intended to stay outside until Riley arrived, but the time seemed to be moving awfully slowly. Standing up, she went back inside.

"No one yet?" she asked, even though she knew no cars had driven up. She looked at the oven time. Five-fifteen.

"Why don't you call her?" her mom suggested. "Find out where she is. What time she'll get here."

Cassie didn't want to. A sick pit formed in her stomach, but she couldn't just walk away and forget she was having a party. She picked up the phone and dialed Riley's number.

"Hello?" Mr. Isabel's gruff voice came over the line.

"Hi, Mr. Isabel," Cassie said. "It's Cassie."

"Hi there, Cassie!" he said, his tone warming. "Riley's not here."

"Well, where is she?" Cassie asked.

"I just dropped her off at Mikaela Reese's party about fifteen minutes ago. Surprised you're not there. She said everyone's going."

"Tonight's my birthday party too," Cassie said. Her ears were ringing and her voice didn't sound right. "She said she was coming here."

Silence reigned on the phone. "Well, I'm really sorry about that, Cassie," Mr. Isabel said finally. "She didn't tell me about that."

Cassie blinked, and hot tears spilled down her cheeks. "Okay," she whispered. "Bye." She hung up, and then she couldn't keep back the sobs. "She's not coming. She went to Mikaela's party."

"Oh, honey." Mrs. Jones went around the counter and wrapped her arms around Cassie. Cassie bawled into her shoulder. The beautiful cake behind her mother caught her eye, and it just made her cry harder. None of her friends would even see it.

CHAPTER THIRTY-ONE
To the Rescue

Mrs. Jones pulled away first, holding Cassie out at arm's length and studying her. "Is there anyone else you can think of that might be able to come? Someone you can call right now?"

Cassie remembered her conversation at lunch. "Maybe Andrea. She said she wasn't going to Mikaela's party."

"Call her. Right now. We'll go get her."

Cassie ran to her room and found her address book under the bed. She thumbed through it, landing on Andrea's name and phone number. She exhaled, pleased with herself for at least collecting names and numbers when she'd moved in. She ran back to the kitchen. "I have her number here."

Her mom stayed close by, offering moral support, while Cassie called.

"Hello?" a woman's voice answered.

"Hi, is Andrea there?" Cassie asked, timid.

"Sure, hold on a moment."

The voice changed, and Andrea said, "Hello?"

"Andrea, it's Cassie. Do you want to come to my party?"

"Right now?"

"Yes. Riley didn't come. She went to Mikaela's party. It's just me." Tears filled her eyes again, choking her words.

"Let me ask my mom, okay?"

Cassie could hear Andrea's end of the muffled conversation. "It's her birthday party but no one showed up. She wants to know if I can come."

"We'll come get you!" Cassie shouted into the phone.

"She said they can come get me. Yeah? Really?" Andrea's voice went back to normal. "My mom says I can go."

"Yes!" Cassie hopped up and down with the phone. "Thank you, thank you, Andrea!"

"Come on," Mrs. Jones said, grabbing her purse and the keys. "Let's go get her."

"Jim!" Mrs. Jones called down the hall. "Cassie and I are leaving for a minute. You and the kids can start on the pizza."

Mr. Jones came out of the bedroom, a puzzled frown on his face. "I thought we were having a party."

"Riley's not coming." Mrs. Jones' words came out clipped and angry, and Cassie didn't miss the look her parents exchanged. "But Cassie has another friend who can come, so we're going to pick her up right now."

Her dad looked at her, his eyes flicking over her face. She could only imagine that she had tears stains on her cheeks and swollen red eyes. "That's good that she has another friend to turn to."

Cassie's mom nodded. "Into the car, Cassie. Everything's going to be fine."

She followed her mom outside. She was just shutting the front door when an unfamiliar four-door car pulled into the circle drive. Even as she watched, the passenger door opened, and Betsy popped out.

"Betsy!" Cassie cried. She'd completely forgotten that she'd invited the other girl.

"I'm here for your party!" Betsy said, running over and hugging Cassie.

Betsy's mom got out of the car, shoving her hands into jacket pockets. "I wasn't going to let her come because she doesn't have a gift. But she was just moping all through dinner, so I said, 'Well, maybe you can just take five dollars.' I hope that's okay. We didn't have any way to call you."

Cassie felt the tears burning her eyes again. "Riley didn't come," she said to Betsy. "We're on our way to get Andrea. She said she can come."

"Thank you so much," Mrs. Jones said to Betsy's mom. "You have no idea. . . ."

Her mom nodded. "Betsy, get your stuff! I'll come get you in the morning."

Cassie held on to Betsy's arm, not willing to let her go. Suddenly she felt like laughing giddily. She wouldn't celebrate her birthday alone.

♥

Andrea was ready when they picked her up, her wavy

reddish-brown hair bouncing around her shoulders as she called out to her mom. "They're here!"

Her mom came to the door, and she and Mrs. Jones talked for a minute while Cassie helped Andrea into the car.

"You know Betsy, right?" she asked Andrea. "She's in Ms. Wade's class. Her mom just brought her over."

"Hi. I'm Andrea."

The two girls greeted each other, and Cassie sat between them, a big smile on her face. They might not be the two people she'd expected, but her party was far from ruined.

Andrea's eyes widened when she saw the cake. "That's amazing! Where did you have it done?"

"My mom did it," Cassie said, as proud as could be. "She can decorate any cake."

"It's so beautiful!" Betsy cooed.

Everyone else had already eaten and was downstairs, but Mr. Jones gathered them back up for cake and ice-cream. No one mentioned Riley's absence, so Cassie assumed they had been briefed.

After a movie, she, Betsy, Andrea, and Emily gathered in her room.

"I can't believe Riley didn't come," Andrea said, finally broaching the topic.

"Where is she?" Emily asked. She sat on the floor, doing a puzzle.

Cassie shrugged. She didn't want to talk about it.

"What's this?" Andrea asked, picking up a small pink book.

"I think it's for messages," Cassie said. "Like autographs at the end of the school year, you know? It came with my address book, but I've never used it." She must've pulled it out from under her bed when she was looking up Andrea's number.

"That's cool," Andrea said. "Come here, Betsy."

Cassie changed into her pajamas while the two girls looked through her autograph book. Then Andrea said, "Here, Cassie."

She handed the book to Cassie with a page opened. Cassie read the words there.

—

We promise that we will always be Cassie's friends, and will never choose someone else over her.
Friends forever,
Betsy and Andrea

Both girls had signed the little book.

Cassie smiled at them. "Thank you. Thank you so much for saving my birthday party."

♥

"So you seem happier, Cassie," Mrs. Talbot said at morning recess on Monday. "How did your weekend work out?"

Cassie sat on the sidewalk, digging through the clovers. She didn't feel like swinging right now. Riley was on the swings, and the two girls hadn't spoken all day. Cassie thought about the friends who had been there for her when her "real" friends hadn't been. "Great. Everything actually went really well."

"And your cat? How is she?"

"Doing great!" she said. "She actually only had one kitten in there. They did a C-section, but it turned out she just had a really big bladder. So they stitched her back together."

"What?" Ms. Dawson burst into laughter. "They cut your cat open for no reason?"

"Yeah. Pretty much."

"Ms. Wade," Ms. Dawson said, wiping at her eyes. "You have to hear this story. Cassie, tell her what you told me."

Cassie did, pleased to be the focus of positive attention.

The teachers were still laughing when they walked back into the building. "You're quite the comedian, Cassie," Ms.

Dawson said. "Maybe you should go into the show business."

"I heard Ms. King might put on a talent show," Ms. Wade said. "You should sign up."

A talent show! That would be amazing. Maybe a comedian act was right up her alley. She could hardly wait for Ms. King to make the announcement.

Episode 6: Reaching Higher

CHAPTER THIRTY-TWO
Science Bee

"I'm so excited you're coming to church with me!" Cassie squeezed Riley's hands and hauled her into the chapel. She still felt betrayed when she thought about how Riley had abandoned her at her birthday party, but she didn't really hold it against Riley. Not anymore, anyway. That was months ago now.

"Sure," Riley said, glancing around at all the faces in the pews. "Mom said we had to go."

Cassie shot Mrs. Isabel a grateful smile, but she didn't seem to notice.

"It's not a very big church, is it?" Riley commented as they sat down.

Cassie thought it seemed plenty big. She shrugged. "I guess that depends." Maybe Riley was used to one of the giant churches, like the one on the corner behind the animal hospital.

Throughout the sermon, Riley fidgeted with a piece of

paper, then her ring, then the hem of her skirt before finally letting out a series of sighs. Cassie glanced at her several times, but since Riley didn't say anything, she shrugged it off. She imagined they looked like total opposites next to each other: Riley with her short, strawberry-blond hair and petite frame, and Cassie with her long dark hair, turquoise glasses, and olive skin. Not to mention, while they'd been the same size at the beginning of the year, Cassie was rapidly outgrowing Riley.

When the sermon ended, Cassie excitedly led her to Sunday School.

"Hello, Sister Garrett," she said as soon as she walked in. "Guess who I brought with me? Riley Isabel!" Cassie beamed with pride. Months ago her teacher had discovered that Riley was on their class role, and Cassie had made it her personal mission to get Riley to church ever since. Today she had finally succeeded.

"Welcome, Riley!" Sister Garrett smiled at her and helped her find a chair. "We're so glad you could join us!"

The lesson was a familiar one to Cassie, about loving your neighbor and treating others as you would want to be treated. She nodded along and supplied answers, all while watching Riley's reactions. Riley answered correctly when called upon and definitely understood the principle.

"What did you think?" Cassie asked as they walked to the car after church. "Did you like it?"

"It was kind of boring," Riley said, wrinkling her nose. She climbed into the passenger seat of her car, next to her mother.

"Oh." Cassie looked down, deflated. She brightened. "Well, it gets better! Come next week, too, it's always different."

"Thanks for the invite, Cassie," Mrs. Isabel said warmly.

"Bye," Riley said, closing her door.

"Bye," Cassie echoed. Then she turned around to find her own mother.

♥

On Monday morning, Cassie stood in line with the rest of her fifth-grade class after morning recess, waiting to file back into the room. Ms. Dawson pressed her finger to her lips and waited for everyone to quiet down.

"All right," she said when it was finally silent. "Let's file in like the almost-sixth-graders that you are."

They all cheered. Just two more months, and they were done with this year. She'd been new at the beginning of the year, having just moved to Arkansas from Texas. Now, nine months later, she felt like she knew everyone and everyone knew her.

Two spaces in front of her in line, Riley turned around and grinned. "Almost sixth-graders, right?"

"Yeah." Cassie nodded.

Ms. Dawson watched while the entire class settled into their school work. Slowly the excited chatter died down, and chairs stopped bumping into the desks. Cassie glanced at the assignment on the board and pulled out her notebook. Around her, her classmates did the same until silence filled the classroom.

Ms. Dawson cleared her throat. "If I could have

everyone's attention, please."

Cassie looked up from her work. Her teacher held up a lined sheet of computer paper. "Ms. King is putting on a talent show at the end of the month. Anyone who wants to participate needs to sign up. Make sure you write down your talent."

A talent show! Cassie straightened up, excited. She'd heard rumors about this already. She loved talent shows. She always participated. But usually she sang, and this time, Cassie felt like doing something different. She tapped her pencil to her lips. What else could she do? A few weeks ago she'd thought she wanted to be a comedian, but she couldn't think of anything funny at the moment. What else was there?

She smiled as an idea came to her. She waited until the sign up sheet stopped at her desk, then she carefully penciled in her name. "Cassandra Jones. Clarinet." She beamed down at the paper. Band practices with her dad had been going extremely well. He'd be so pleased with her desire to play the clarinet in the show.

She finished her assignment and pulled out a book to read, hoping to get a few paragraphs in before Ms. Dawson gave them something else to do.

An office helper came into the room and handed a note to the teacher. Ms. Dawson scanned it and looked up.

"Cassandra. Mrs. Holland wants to see you."

Cassie frowned. She'd only met Mrs. Holland once, when she'd thought about joining the Odyssey of the Mind team. That aspiration hadn't lasted long, and Cassie had never spoken to Mrs. Holland again. What did she want now? Cassie closed her book and stuck it in her desk.

Mrs. Holland was instructing a small group of kids when Cassie knocked on the open classroom door.

"Oh, hold on, Cassandra." She put down the dry erase marker and grabbed a pack of papers off her desk. Then she came to the doorway. "You know, we could've really used you during the Odyssey of the Mind competition. You just didn't want to?"

Cassie shrugged. She didn't feel like explaining that she hadn't felt capable of the challenges. Or that the other team members hadn't exactly welcomed her.

"That's okay. Sometimes it just doesn't work out, doesn't fit in our schedules." She held the packet of paper out to Cassie. "We have Science Olympiad coming up this month, and we're putting together teams this week. I'd like you to be on one of them."

Cassie just blinked at her and pushed her glasses up on her nose, not even touching the paper. "Um, I don't do so well on teams." What she meant was, she was the last one picked for everything.

"No? Well, there are some individual competitions. Take a look." She shook the papers slightly. "Go through and pick out the things that interest you. There's bound to be something. Then have your mom sign the permission slip, and we'll start practicing this week."

Mrs. Holland wasn't showing any sign of taking the papers back. Hesitantly, Cassie took them from her. "I'll look through it," she said, hoping that didn't sound like a commitment.

"Perfect. We'll see you later in the week."

♥

"There look like some fun activities in here, Cassie." Her mom flipped through the packet after dinner.

Cassie didn't look up from her math homework. She hadn't looked through the packet. The experience she'd had with the "teams" during the Odyssey of the Mind challenges had been enough for her. She had no desire to participate in anything like that again. "I thought you didn't like all the time commitment and stuff."

"This isn't the same, Cassie. All the practices are during school. All the events take place on one day. It's an all-day thing."

"All day?" Cassie repeated. "Like a Saturday?"

Mrs. Jones pulled a pocket calendar from her purse. "No, it's a Friday. Like a field trip."

Well, the idea had merit, at least. She'd get out of class to practice and then miss an entire day of school for the competition.

Right. The competition. She shook her head. "I never win stuff. I'm the kid no one wants to play with."

"Oh, honey, that's not true. Look here." Mrs. Jones shoved the math homework to the side and spread out the papers. "Several events run every hour, so you choose which ones you want to do. Like a paper airplane competition."

Cassie laughed. She'd never mastered paper airplanes.

"Or building volcanoes. Or, look, Cassie, playing a song

on music bottles!"

"What?" That intrigued her. Cassie loved music. She read through the description. It was an individual event. "I might be able to do that." She felt the stirrings of excitement as she read through some of the other contests. "There's a spelling bee. I'm good at spelling!"

"Exactly." Her mom settled back with a smile. "You can do this. I'm signing it."

The next day Cassie took the paper to Mrs. Holland before school started. It was signed, and she'd written down the events she wanted to participate in.

"Fantastic, Cassandra. I'll send someone to get you out of class today for our practice. We meet every Tuesday and Thursday."

"Okay. Great." Cassie offered a smile, hoping she looked more confident than she felt.

A different kid brought a note today, and this time five kids got up and left Ms. Dawson's room.

"You're joining us this time, Cassie?" Emmett asked. He'd sat next to her all year. He was the one who had tried to get Cassie to do Odyssey of the Mind in the fall, and even though Cassie backed out, he'd never held it against her.

"Yeah, I think so," she said. "It doesn't look that hard." And didn't require as much time commitment.

"You'll do great!" he said.

Not everyone thought so.

"Her again!" Jerry scowled when she walked in with the group from her class. "She made our team worse last time! I'm not working with her!"

Some of the kids tittered with laughter, but Mrs. Holland hushed them. "Jerry, that's a horrible way to treat someone. Cassie probably doesn't want to be on your team, either."

Cassie definitely did not. She did not want to be anywhere near him.

"That being said," Mrs. Holland continued, "many of you did sign up for events that require a partner. I'll let you know who else signed up, and you can choose from those people."

She started going through some of the activities that hadn't interested Cassie, listing off the people who signed up. Then she said, "Science spelling bee. Cassandra Jones, Sanderson Cox, Jerry Freeman, and Brenna Atkins."

"No way am I pairing up with either of those girls," Jerry said. "Bunch of geeks." He leaned his chair back and looked at another boy across the room. "Sanderson, man!"

Sanderson leaned back too and gave him a thumbs up.

Cassie looked around for Brenna. Brenna was in her class, but Cassie didn't know her very well. She spotted her at another table, her arms folded across her chest. She had shoulder-length, frizzy blond hair, and colorful plastic glasses frames like Cassie. Cassie waved at her, tried to get her attention, but she just sat there with a scowl on her face.

"All right, that's done," Mrs. Holland said. "Let's start with your first event. Stations are set up around the room. If you can't remember what you signed up for, go check your paper. Up, we only have ten more minutes of class!"

CHAPTER THIRTY-THREE

Tears and Hugs

"Mother's Day is in two weeks," Ms. Dawson said, handing each student an empty two-liter soda bottle. "To go along with our studies on plants and energy, we're going to make miniature greenhouses."

Cassie accepted the green bottle with curiosity and eagerness. How was this going to turn into a greenhouse?

"Have you ever done this before?" she asked Emmett, watching as he started to cut his bottle at the bottom.

"Yeah," he said, nodding. "It was an Odyssey of the Mind project a few years ago."

"Oh." Which meant she would be absolutely horrible at this. She scowled, remembering Brenna and their unsuccessful practice for Science Olympiad.

As if reading her mind, Emmett added, "This is really easy. You just add the dirt and seeds and leave it in the sun."

By the time Cassie had followed Ms. Dawson's directions

and set her bottle/green house in the window sill, she had hope that Emmett was right. She thought what a lovely surprise that would be for Mother's Day. Of course, her mom did have a tendency to kill all the plants she tried to grow. Cassie frowned. Maybe there was someone else she could give it to.

♥

By Thursday, Cassie was feeling much more confident with her chosen activities for Science Olympiad. The bottle music consisted of soda bottles filled with water. Each one played a different note when she blew across the top of it. The water level dictated what the note would be. It wasn't hard, and she felt good about it.

The Spelling Bee wasn't as agreeable. Or rather, her partner wasn't as agreeable. Brenna didn't want to practice with her and refused to spell words when Cassie threw them at her. When it was Cassie's turn to spell, she'd make noises or say "time!" over and over again. It frustrated Cassie to no end, and she wished she could just do the event by herself.

"One more week, guys!" Mrs. Holland said as they filed out. "Next Friday is our competition!"

Cassie chattered nonstop about Science Olympiad with her sister Emily on the bus.

"It sounds like fun," Emily said. "I want to do it too."

"Maybe when you're in fourth grade," Cassie said superiorly. "They don't have any third graders doing it."

They walked the quarter mile from the bus to their house.

"There's Mom," Scott, Cassie's six-year-old brother, said.

Sure enough, Mrs. Jones sat on the porch steps between two of the four white pillars in front of the house. She was usually inside, making dinner or sewing or folding laundry when they got home. Cassie couldn't think of the last time she'd met them outside.

"Hi, kids," she greeted, the corners of her mouth drawing down. "Everyone go in and sit on the couch, okay? I have something important to talk to you about."

Mrs. Jones' expression was ominous. Cassie tried to read her eyes. This was serious, but maybe it wasn't bad. It could just be life-changing. Like, maybe her mom was pregnant. Hope flared for a second. Cassie would love another brother or sister. But just as quickly, that hope dissipated. There was no glimmer of excitement in her mother's face, no quiver of barely contained joy around her mouth.

"What is it?" Cassie asked, not moving from the front porch.

"Go sit on the couch, please. I'm coming too."

Cassie sat next to Annette and Emily. She clasped her hands in her lap and held very still, trying not to be nervous about whatever it was her mom had to say.

Mrs. Jones came in and stood in front of them. "This pertains to all of you," she said, "but to you most of all, Cassie." She trained her gaze on Cassie. Taking a deep breath, she said, "Scaredy was hit by a car today. He's dead."

The world tilted. Cassie thought her mom was saying something else, but she couldn't focus. Her ears rang. "Wait," she said. "I don't understand. How do you know he's dead?" She stood up. "I need to see him."

"Cassie." Tears glistened in her mom's eyes. "He's dead, honey. I had to—I had to clean up the body."

No. Cassie shook her head. Not her sweet Scaredy, with his skinny little tail and the way he always got in her lap

when she sat on the floor. "He can't be dead," she gasped out, a sob building in her stomach. "I didn't even say bye this morning." The cry burst out of her, gaining momentum. It stole her breath, and Cassie put her hands on her knees, quick little sobs escaping with each gulp of air. "No, no, no. No!"

"Come here, sweetie." Her mom held out her arms, but Cassie didn't move from the couch. She curled around herself, a physical ache spreading from her chest to her shoulders and down her arms. The noises escaping her didn't even sound human. She pressed her hands to her mouth, but it did nothing to muffle the ragged gasps.

Beside her, she was vaguely aware of her brother and sisters crying too, but their grief couldn't possibly compare to hers. Scaredy was her dog. Riley gave him to her. She had loved him, and he had loved her.

What would she do now? How could she possibly continue on alone?

CHAPTER THIRTY-FOUR
Time Not Slipping

No amount of comfort or consolation eased the pain. Cassie sat at the dinner table with tears rolling down her cheeks. She bit her lip several times to stop the whimpers that crept through.

"It was just a dog, Cassie," her dad said, losing patience. "Everyone else is done crying."

Cassie lowered her head and stared at her plate, covered in food her mom hoped she would eat. She had no response for her father. She only knew the awful pain she felt in her whole body, the loss of a soul, a kindred spirit.

"Jim, she loved that dog," Mrs. Jones said. "Let her mourn."

He grunted. "Well, not at the dinner table."

Cassie backed her chair away. "I just want to lie down anyway."

No one stopped her as she went to her room. She collapsed on her bed and closed her eyes, willing sleep to come. Surely at least in her sleep she would find relief.

♥

Cassie opened her eyes when her alarm went off. She wondered why they felt so sticky, so stiff she could hardly move them. She rolled over onto her side, the heavy feeling of dread thick in her chest, but she couldn't remember why. "Scaredy?" She sat up in bed and reached toward her feet, feeling for the dog's warmth. "Scaredy?" She clucked her tongue.

"He's dead, Cassie." Emily stumbled to the wall and flipped on the light.

The sensation of loss washed over Cassie. "He's dead?" she whispered. It had happened. The night before came flooding back. She took several deep breaths, trying to control the pain before the tears could overflow.

She wasn't successful. Cassie put her face in her hands to muffle the sounds of her crying.

"Cassie?" Emily leaned toward her. "Can I help you?"

Cassie shook her head. No one could help her.

Her mom was up with them, which was unusual. Cassie was responsible for getting everyone to the bus, and if there was a problem, her dad was generally around, getting ready for work. Mrs. Jones came into the bathroom as Cassie pulled her long hair into a ponytail.

"How are you, honey?" she asked, tucking a few strands behind Cassie's ears.

Cassie shrugged, keeping her eyes on her reflection. She couldn't speak, or the dam of emotions would break.

Her mother wrapped her arms around her from behind

and kissed her cheek. "I know you loved him, Cassie. I'm so sorry."

Cassie's nostrils flared and her eyes reddened. Her face crumpled, and she turned into her mother, sobbing. She missed him already. She wouldn't have to rush out the door anymore to make sure he didn't sneak out with her, or ask her dad to take him for a walk because she'd forgotten to.

Mrs. Jones brushed a stray piece of hair from Cassie's face. "You've got to go to the bus. Will you be okay at school today?"

She nodded, dropping her eyes so her mother wouldn't see her uncertainty. She had no idea how she'd be.

❤

She found out soon enough. She sat on the back of the bus and stared out the window so she could cry without anyone noticing her. But as soon as she got off, everyone noticed.

"Cassie, have you been crying?" Betsy, another fifth-grader who rode the bus with Cassie, took her by the arm and peered into her face.

"Our dog died," Emily said, turning around to look at them. She pulled her face into a grimace. "We're all sad about it."

Cassie's eyes burned, and she pressed the palm of her hand to her head. *Her* dog. Her dog died.

"I'm so sorry!" Betsy hugged her. She hovered over Cassie protectively as they walked through the halls toward the fifth-grade corridor. Cassie heard her shooing people away, whispering hurried explanations. She took her to Ms.

Dawson's door and led her inside. "Where's your desk, Cassie?"

Cassie pointed, and Betsy helped her sit down.

"I'll see you after school, okay?" Betsy said, crouching in front of her.

Cassie nodded, grateful for her help, but feeling more numb than anything else. Betsy said a few words to Ms. Dawson, and then again to Riley and Andrea as they walked into the classroom.

"Scaredy died?" Riley stood in front of Cassie's desk, her own expression falling. "How could you let him die?"

"Riley!" Andrea shoved her away. "Cassie, I'm so sorry about your dog."

Cassie couldn't even feel any self-indignation over Riley's accusation. It pierced her heart like a dagger, and she wondered if this was her fault. If she hadn't let Scaredy spend so much time outside . . . if she had skipped school yesterday . . .

As if reading her thoughts, Andrea added, "There was nothing you could do to change it."

Riley went to her desk, her fair skin splotchy, wiping tears away with her hands.

"Thank you, Andrea," Cassie whispered. Andrea and Betsy had come to Cassie's rescue at her birthday party, showing up when no one else had. She knew they were true friends.

Ms. Dawson started class, but Cassie barely heard her. She stared at the clock behind the white board. The minute-hand didn't move. The second-hand continued to rotate round and round, but time seemed to be holding still. She took a shuddering breath, feeling the thud of each heartbeat, the ache in her chest, the pain that wouldn't go away. She willed time to move forward. For years to pass by so that she wouldn't feel this pain anymore. She didn't want to be here without her dog.

A couple of kids gathered around the windowsill after recess, checking out the soda-bottle greenhouses. Cassie didn't care. She sat down at her desk and stared at the corner.

"Yours is growing the best, Cassie," Matthew said, taking his seat across from her and smiling. She wasn't sure if all her classmates had been told about her dog or if he just sensed her mood, but Matthew had been extra nice today.

"Great," she mumbled, averting her eyes.

❤

Cassie stepped off the bus and took three steps before she remembered that Scaredy wouldn't be greeting her here anymore. She stopped and gasped, breathing hard to control the tears that threatened. By the time she got home, she was crying, sucking in short little breaths and wiping her cheeks.

She came in last, closing the front door behind her. She could hear voices in the kitchen, but she didn't feel inclined to join them. Leaving her backpack on the floor, she went to her room and lay on the bed. She wrapped her arms around her torso and stared at the wall, tears silently rolling down her cheeks, over her nose, into her ear.

A few minutes later, her mom came in and rubbed her

back. "How was school, honey?"

"Fine," Cassie mumbled.

"Good." Her mom took a deep breath. "I need your help this weekend."

"With what?" Cassie whispered, still not looking at her mother.

"Your dad and I were invited to a special banquet in Siloam. We'll be gone overnight."

Now Cassie rolled over, a glimmer of interest sparking in her chest. "You're leaving me in charge all weekend?"

A smile graced her mother's lips. "No, sweetie. Your dad's picking up Grandma on the way home, and she'll stay with you. But I rely on you to keep things under control."

Cassie groaned and pressed her hands into her face. "Can't you find someone besides Grandma?" Grandma had a stroke in her twenties, and her moods and behavior were erratic. She'd only moved to Arkansas a month ago to be closer to her son, Cassie's father, but Cassie wished she'd move away again. Sometimes when she came over, all she did was yell and swat everyone on the bum. Other times she only wanted fried chicken for every meal. Her favorite movies were black and white, and she sent everyone to bed if there was any noise during "I Love Lucy."

"It was very last-minute, Cassie. I hope you'll help and not give her a hard time."

"She gives me a hard time!" She couldn't imagine anything worse for this weekend than to be stuck with Grandma.

A car rumbled over the gravel outside, and her mom

stood up. "That's your dad now. Come on out and say hi."

Cassie folded her arms over her chest and huffed after her mother, not at all happy by this turn of events.

Grandma had already come into the house, her tiny feet clicking across the tile in her four-inch heels. She gave Cassie a disapproving look when she spotted her.

"I hope you didn't wear your hair like that at school," she said, peering at Cassie over the tips of her glasses.

Cassie reached up and felt her ponytail. What was wrong with it?

"Mom," her dad said, taking her by the elbow, "Karen and I are getting ready to go. I think she already set water to boil on the stove so you can make macaroni and cheese."

"Yay!" Annette said, following behind and clinging to her dad's leg. "That's my favorite!"

"I'll make something much better than that," Grandma said.

"Jim, I'm taking my stuff out to the car," her mom called after her dad. She cast a look at Cassie. "Be patient with her, okay? And helpful."

Cassie nodded. She waited until her mom and dad had left before shutting herself in the bathroom.

No sooner had Cassie sat down on the toilet seat than she remembered the days when Scaredy first arrived and was too afraid of anyone to leave the bathroom. He'd cowered behind the toilet until Cassie finally earned his trust. Fresh tears seeped out of the corners of her eyes. He'd loved her like he'd loved no one else.

The door barged open, and Cassie jumped off the toilet

seat in surprise, glad she hadn't actually been using the bathroom. "Grandma!" she exclaimed. "You're not supposed to come in when I'm in here!" Her parents had rules about not locking the bathroom door, but they also had rules about respecting someone else's privacy.

"You've been in here too long," her grandmother said. "It's time for dinner."

Cassie's lip trembled, and she sucked in a breath, trying to compose herself. For all she knew, Grandma would make fun of her for crying. "I'm not feeling well. I think I'll just go to bed."

"You can't stay in the bathroom moping all evening," her grandma said. "You think I can't see you've been crying? Everyone else is eating."

Cassie doubted she would eat even if she weren't upset. It smelled like her grandma had made hash, the name she used for anything involving potatoes and eggs. "I can't eat. I'm going to throw up." She made a noise in the back of her throat.

Her grandma made a face. "Fine, but don't get up in an hour expecting food. It's now or never. And your mom told you to help me."

"Ask Emily," Cassie said, in no mood to humor her grandmother. "She's just as capable."

"Probably more so," Grandma agreed. "More responsible."

"Go ask her, then," Cassie said. *And leave me alone.* At least Emily's ability to be the best at everything had its benefits.

Grandma left the bathroom, and Cassie stumbled off to her bed. She sobbed into her blanket until her eyes were too sore to cry anymore and her head pounded like someone was swinging a hammer into one side every few seconds. She lay there in misery until exhaustion made it impossible to keep thinking.

CHAPTER THIRTY-FIVE

Homecooking

No dog pulling at her blankets woke Cassie in the morning, but her body felt over-saturated with sleep, and she couldn't stay in bed past six. She went to the bathroom and washed her face, feeling more invigorated than the day before. The guest room where Grandma slept was on the other side of the house, past the kitchen. Grandma didn't like to get up early, either, so for now Cassie's time was her own.

She put on a sweater and stepped outside into the crisp morning air. Crazy, because she knew by mid-afternoon it would be too hot for pants. She shoved her hands in her pockets and took a deep breath, waiting for the tears to come. They didn't. Instead she just felt calm and accepting.

She headed toward the road, wanting to see the place where Scaredy had been hit. She couldn't imagine the type of person who would run over someone's dog and just keep going. He couldn't stop and say sorry? Ask about the dog he'd just killed?

A dark spot stained the road a few feet from the yard, but that was the only indication of the tragedy. Her mom had told her how she scrubbed it to clean it up before they got home from school. How she'd cried the whole time, tears rolling off the tip of her nose and into her mouth.

Cassie knelt at the stain and pressed her fingers into it. A few loose pieces of gravel tumbled away from her. She picked up one of the small rocks and examined it. It had a darker tint to it, though she had no idea if it was blood or just the natural color.

A breeze blew past her face, whispering into her ear. Cassie closed her eyes and lifted her head toward the sun. Her heart beat a little harder, and she felt quite certain that it was no ordinary wind. She opened her eyes again and peered down at the little rock in her hand. This held a piece of her dog. Here was a remnant of him.

She stuck it in her pocket, and the tears came now, greedy in their desire to remind her of her loss. She wiped at them, trying to find again the peace she'd felt when she came outside.

❤

Grandma didn't make the day any easier, but Cassie supposed maybe that was a good thing. By the time she came inside from her morning walk, Grandma was up, and she was furious that Cassie had gone out alone, without permission.

"I'm eleven years old," Cassie said in the face of the verbal onslaught. "I can go for a walk when I feel like it."

"Not without getting permission, young lady!" Grandma said, shaking her finger in Cassie's face.

"Sure I can," Cassie said, not about to back down. "My mom lets me. I just tell her I'm going outside. Sometimes I don't even do that." Which wasn't exactly true.

"I'm not your mother, am I!" Her grandmother reached down and swatted Cassie's bum. "When I'm here, you obey my rules!"

Cassie's face burned with humiliation. Her dad didn't even spank her anymore. She huffed away from her grandmother and threw herself into her chores, staying out of sight. The anger and resentment, at least, gave her something to chafe at other than her aching heart.

They succeeded in having macaroni and cheese for dinner only because Emily made it before Grandma had a chance to intervene. Apparently put out by that, she nagged them all at dinner about how bad the meal was for them and how they'd all get fat someday.

"Look at you, Cassie," she said. "Already not fitting properly in your clothes. And is that a training bra I see? Better watch it, girl, you're going to be fat."

Scott snickered, and Cassie refused to give in to the bullying. "Some girls at school already wear bras. They're much larger than me."

"Maybe you're behind, then. Maybe your body doesn't get enough nutrients to grow effectively."

Ugh. Cassie rolled her eyes. "Whatever, Grandma."

"Don't talk back to me, young lady," her grandmother said. "Or you'll be excused from the table."

"I'm not hungry, anyway," Cassie said, pushing her chair back. She knew she'd regret her outburst when her mom got home; Grandma would tell on her, and her mom would chastise her for not being more "helpful."

She let herself onto the deck. Baby Blue stood up in one of the corners and stretched. Her black kitten came out from behind her and rubbed against Cassie's leg. Cassie scratched behind his ears and looked out over the yard. Where were the dogs? She rested her elbows on the railing. "Pioneer!" she shouted. "Scaredy!"

She only had to wait a moment before she heard the clatter of dog claws on the wooden stairs. Pioneer's head popped over the top of the staircase a moment later, and Cassie gathered him into her arms, shoving her fingers into his shaggy fur. She stood up again, scanning for her smaller dog. "Scaredy!" she shouted. "Sca—" her voice strangled as her throat suddenly closed. He wouldn't come. He wouldn't ever come again. She sat down on the deck and burst into tears. She buried her head in Pioneer's shoulder, clinging to him.

♥

"I'm sorry things didn't go so well with Grandma," Cassie said to her mom Sunday afternoon as Mrs. Jones helped her put away the dishes after church.

Cassie hadn't come out of her room Saturday even after she heard her grandmother get in the car with her dad and leave. Her mom came in to check on her, but Cassie kept her eyes closed and pretended to be asleep. To be honest, she'd been afraid her mom would yell at her for back-talking Grandma.

But this morning, when Cassie got up and started to get ready for church, not only did her mom not bring it up, but Cassie felt amazingly better. Several times throughout the day she forced herself to think about Scaredy. She waited for the agony to prick her heart, the tears to well up in her eyes. But while she'd felt an achy, hollowness in her chest, it wasn't enough to draw tears.

"Oh, honey, I know how difficult she is." She gave Cassie a stern look. "I expect better of you, though. You're eleven. You should know when to bite your tongue and let it go."

Cassie nodded. "I know." She did, too. She should've been more mature. Grandma wouldn't be, after all.

"She'll be spending Mother's Day with us. I hope you'll behave."

Cassie groaned. "Of course I will."

"You seem better today," her mom added, putting away the last plate and facing Cassie. "How are you dealing?"

Cassie blinked, but no moisture stung her eyes. She laid the forks in their spots, lining them up nicely. "Good, I think. I'll always miss him." She didn't feel like crying anymore, though. "He was a happy dog."

Her mom gave her a hug. "You'll make it through this."

CHAPTER THIRTY-SIX
Science Olympiad

The school week crawled by. Friday finally arrived, and Cassie tapped her foot impatiently against the floor during morning announcements. She kept checking her watch or the clock on the wall, willing it to hurry up. She knew they wouldn't dismiss for Science Olympiad until after P.E., but it seemed like that time would never arrive.

Finally, right in the middle of grading each other's math homework, the intercom buzzed to life.

"Teachers, please excuse those students participating in Science Olympiad. Their bus will be leaving now," the familiar office voice said.

"Goodbye," Ms. Dawson said, and Cassie jumped up, along with Emmett, Brenna, and a few other kids.

"Yes, this rocks!" Emmett said, pumping his fists as they hurried down the hall. He walked backwards and gave everyone a thumbs up. "I love Science Olympiad!"

Cassie giggled with the others, her body humming with

an excited, nervous energy. She'd been practicing her bottle music skills all week, judging how much water to put in the bottle, recognizing the important notes.

The Science Spelling Bee, however, was another story. She cast a sideways glance at Brenna, who walked along with both arms taking advantage of their full range of motion, one pumping by her ear while the other brushed her thigh, and then switching. Cassie grimaced. The two of them did not get along, and she didn't know how they would do this spelling bee together. She supposed they didn't have to be friends as long as they could spell correctly. But every time they practiced, Brenna insisted she was spelling it wrong, and they rarely got a word completely spelled before the timer went off.

Certainly it wouldn't be that bad during the actual event.

They road a bus to another school. Several other buses already crowded the parking lot, with students streaming toward the school. Cassie and her classmates followed them. They gathered in a big auditorium and scattered around the bleachers.

"You're going to love this, Cassie," Emmett said. "It's so fun."

Jerry said something then, and Emmett turned his attention away from her. A balding man in a suit stepped up to the microphone.

"Welcome to Science Olympiad!" he boomed.

The kids cheered, Cassie with them.

"This is where you get to invent, to push your mind to its limits, to see what you're really capable of!" He went on to talk about what an amazing group they were, but Cassie was already thinking about her two main events. Her foot began its nervous tap against the floor. She pulled her schedule out of her bag. Bottle Music was at one o'clock and the spelling bee at three.

Everyone clapped, and Cassie looked up to see the man sitting back down and a group of kids walking out onto the floor. She tensed. Was she supposed to be with them? But no, a quick perusal showed they weren't from her school.

"You really ought to pay more attention, Cassandra," she scolded herself.

The kids put on a skit that was probably supposed to be funny. Or maybe they just hoped it would be funny. The students around Cassie tittered politely, but from where she sat, Cassie could hardly even hear the jokes.

The balding man stood up again. "All right, students. Everyone should be scheduled for an event every hour. The noon competitions start in ten minutes! If you need help, we have tables by the doors to direct you. You're free to go!"

Cassie's heart gave a little lurch in her chest. He had to be wrong. An event every hour? Mrs. Holland had signed her up for two events. She climbed down the bleachers and made her way to the tables pressed against the wall.

"Hi, I'm just trying to see what events I'm signed up for," she said to the friendly-looking woman behind the table. She clutched her backpack to her chest, hoping she didn't look as nervous as she felt.

"Name?" the woman asked, shuffling some papers in

front of her.

"Cassandra Jones."

"Cassandra." She ran her finger down the list and paused at her name. "Let's see, right now you have Paper Airplanes."

Her stomach did a somersault. "What?"

"First you have Paper Airplanes."

Cassie waved a hand. She'd heard the lady; she just couldn't believe it. She tightened her grip on her backpack. How could Mrs. Holland do this to her? She couldn't fold paper to save her life! "And then?"

"Bottle Music at one."

Cassie nodded. At least that was right.

"Then Chemical Reactions at two."

Cassie forced her head to bob up and down in acknowledgment. Why hadn't someone told her she had to be signed up for an event every hour?

"And then the Science Spelling Bee at three."

"So where do I go first?" Cassie whispered, her throat suddenly dry. Did she really have to do this? Would she get in trouble if she just didn't show up?

"Here's a map. You go down the hall, turn right, and it's room two-oh-three."

"Thanks." Cassie threaded her arms through her backpack and held the map in front of her. She stopped outside room two-oh-three and peered inside.

One or two girls stood amidst fifteen or so boys. Cassie groaned. This was so the wrong event.

"Oh, you do paper airplanes?" a voice said at her

shoulder.

Cassie turned around. A boy stood there. He gave her a grin, his brown eyes bright behind wire-framed glasses. She'd seen him before at practice, so she knew he was from her school, but they'd never spoken.

"Come on, let's go in," he said, gesturing with his head.

Cassie didn't feel like she had any choice but to follow. He sat down at a desk with a white sheet of paper on it. He picked up his paper and started folding it. She sat next to him and slowly mimicked his actions.

"I'm Miles. I don't think we've actually met before."

"I'm Cassie," she said, hoping he didn't notice that she had no idea what to do.

"Okay, let's get started!" a teacher at the front of the room said. "The three airplanes that fly the farthest win. Everyone gets two tries. Make your first airplane!"

Miles stopped talking and concentrated on making his plane, his eyebrows furrowing toward the bridge of his nose as he focused. Cassie bent her paper as quickly as she could, but Miles was too fast to follow. He stood up and joined the line of kids ready to throw their plane.

"Just get it over with," Cassie muttered. She got in line behind him.

"Oh, hey," he said, then turned back to watch the competition.

Her stomach knotted up. In a moment, he'd know she was a fraud, not even a real paper airplane mechanic.

CHAPTER THIRTY-SEVEN
Of Aeroplanes

Miles threw his airplane, leaning forward as it glided through the air. His shoulders relaxed as it slid closer to the other airplanes, and then a pleased smile pushed his lips upward as it flew past.

"Yes," he said, pumping his fists.

Cassandra was the only person who hadn't gone yet. Miles turned toward her.

"Your turn," he said.

Her heart thumped so hard in her throat that she couldn't breathe. Cassie stepped forward, aimed her crumpled paper, and threw. It arced upward at nearly a ninety-degree angle before taking a nose-dive and crashing a few inches in front of her.

The other kids hooted and laughed. Cassie's face burned, and she swallowed back tears. She fought the urge to run from the room.

"Round two," the teacher said, and the kids started on

their next airplane. Cassie returned to her seat, keeping her eyes lowered.

"Hey, Cassie," Miles said.

She didn't look at him, certain he'd just make fun of her too.

"Cassie," he whispered, leaning closer.

"What?" Cassie bent her paper in half and stared at it.

"You don't know how to make an airplane, huh? Here." He took her paper from her. "Let me help you."

Cassie looked at him, a flush of gratitude warming her. She didn't say a word as he twisted and folded her paper into a master plane.

"It'll fly better this time," he said, giving her a smile as he handed it back. Then he started crafting his own.

"Thank you," she said, not sure what else to say. She turned it over in her hands, admiring it. "I just throw it?"

He laughed. "How did you end up in this class?"

"Mrs. Holland signed me up for it," she grumbled. "I didn't even know."

"Kind of funny," he said.

She didn't think so. The kids were lining up again, and she joined them, her heart rate already climbing. Miles had built her plane, but what if she needed skills to throw it properly?

"Go on," Miles whispered, prodding her forward. "You go first."

Cassie took a deep, shaky breath, hoping it would steady her hand. No such luck. The paper trembled in her grip. She pulled her arm back and threw it forward. The airplane glided along the same path as the others, coming to rest several feet in front of her. Cassie exhaled in relief.

"Good job," Miles said. He stepped up to the line and threw his own plane. It went much farther than Cassie's had, even though the design looked equal to her untrained eyes.

Cassie didn't care. Not only had she managed to complete the event with dignity, but she'd made a friend.

"Where are you off to next?"

Miles exited the room behind Cassie, holding a certificate in his hand that said "second place."

"Bottle Music," Cassie answered, her cheeks warming. This was the event she felt confident in, and yet suddenly she felt sheepish. Was it dumb to know how to play music on bottles filled with water?

"Oh," Miles said, cocking his head to the side. "I like music."

"Yeah?" Cassie relaxed. He wasn't going to make fun of her. "My dad directs a band at school. You should join us."

"Nah, I just like to sing." He gave her a wave. "Good luck. See you in school."

"Bye." Cassie waved back and followed her map to the next classroom. She walked in, glad to see no one else inside. "Hello?" she called out, looking for the teacher.

"Hello!" Mrs. King came around a corner, the music teacher from her own elementary school. "Hi, Cassie! I'm so pleased to see you. I was happy to see your name on the sign up list! You're so good with music."

Cassie warmed under the praise. Mrs. King always made

her feel talented. "Hi. I didn't know you were the teacher in charge of this event."

"Yep." She put seven empty glass bottles on a table. "You're the only person signed up for this hour. Ready?"

Cassie nodded and put her backpack down. "Ready." She took the pitcher of water and filled the first water bottle. She'd be able to judge the water level of each seceding bottle after that. Putting the pitcher down, she leaned over and blew across the top. The pitch wasn't exactly right. She added a smidgen more of water, then blew again. She needed an A, but it sounded too low. She added a little bit more and tried again. There. That was the sound she needed.

Cassie glanced at the piano against the wall. She badly wanted to hit the note on the keys, but she'd lose points if she did. She had to trust her ear. But if her A was off, the rest of the scale would be, too.

She crossed her mental fingers and filled the next bottle. Using the first one as her judging point, she blew across it until she got what sounded like a B. She continued with the rest of the bottles. When she blew across the last one, she hoped the note was actually a G and didn't just sound like it to her.

"Marvelous!" Mrs. King clapped her hands and smiled. "Perfect score, Cassie!"

Cassie straightened up, satisfaction warming her chest. Between Bottle Music and Miles, the day wasn't a total loss, after all.

❤

Cassie stepped into the room for the spelling bee at three o'clock. Six other kids were already seated around desks. A quick glance around showed no sign of Brenna. Maybe she wouldn't show? That might not be such a bad thing. Faking it through the last event had exhausted Cassie.

She sat down at an empty desk and folded her hands in front of her. A woman came in with a folder and checked the clock.

"All right, let's get started." Her eyes landed on Cassie, and she frowned. "Where's your partner, doll?"

"Right here." Brenna burst in, her frizzy blond hair flying around her head, crumpled papers bursting out of her backpack. She seated herself next to Cassie and faced the front without a word. "Ready."

"Perfect." The woman nodded. "I'm Ms. Lech, and I'll call the words out to you. You'll confer together about the spelling and one of you will spell it out. If your team gets it right, you get two points. If the team before you can't spell their word, it will get passed to your team for one point. Let me make sure I've got the teams right." She called them out. Satisfied that they were all present, she began.

The first few words weren't too hard. Cassie even knew the ones that the other teams had to spell, and she began to relax. Maybe it wouldn't matter that she didn't like her partner.

"Cassie and Brenna," Ms. Lech said, "canoeing."

"Do you know it?" Brenna hissed.

Cassie shook her head. "No. I know how to spell canoe."

Brenna wrote it out on a piece of paper. "So if we drop

the E and add the ING, it looks like this."

Cassie read the word. C-A-N-O-I-N-G. "That can't be right. It looks like cano-ing."

"One minute left," Ms. Lech said.

Brenna crossed out the O as well.

"Caning?" Cassie said skeptically.

Brenna crumpled up the paper and tossed it to the ground. "Well, what are your suggestions?"

Cassie didn't have any, really.

"Ten seconds, ladies."

"Just say something," Brenna hissed.

"Canoeing," Cassie blurted. "C-A-N-U-I-N-G." Ugh, that was wrong, she just knew it. Nothing about it fit.

"That is incorrect. Next team?"

The girl cleared her throat and sat up straighter. "Canoeing. C-A-N-O-E-I-N-G."

"That is correct."

Cassie groaned. Of course. Just like it sounded. She and Brenna were down by two points now. "What does canoeing have to do with science, anyway?" she grumbled.

"Huh," Brenna agreed. Probably the closest thing to a decent conversation they'd ever had.

The next few words weren't difficult, and she and Brenna climbed back up. Soon they were in second place again.

"Okay, this is the last round," Ms. Lech said. "These are the ones that count for two points, regardless of who gets it right. Team one. Kinetic."

They hunched over and debated for several seconds, and then the boy member said, "Kinetic. C-H-E-N-E-T-I-C.

Kinetic."

"I'm sorry, that's incorrect. Team two?"

Cassie sat up straighter. That was them. If they could get this extra point, they'd be in first place. "How do we spell this, Brenna?"

"Okay." Brenna had her paper out already. "K. C." She wrote down "cenetic."

"No, that looks like cinema," Cassie said, shaking her head.

"Okay, okay." Brenna tried again. "Kenetic."

Cassie slapped the table. "That's it!"

Brenna cleared her throat. "Kinetic. K-E-N-E-T-I-C."

"I'm sorry, that's incorrect. Team three?"

Cassie listened as they got it wrong as well. Team four finally spelled it correctly, bumping them into second place, and Cassie shook her head. "Off by one letter."

The round ended, and she and Brenna were in third place.

Brenna shrugged as she took their certificate. "We didn't do too bad."

There were only four teams. "Yeah," Cassie agreed. "It wasn't so bad."

CHAPTER THIRTY-EIGHT
Dominoes Rule

Cassie knocked on Ms. Buckley's office door. She glanced down at the note the office runner had delivered to Ms. Dawson's room.

Please send Cassandra Jones to Ms. Buckley's room.

The door opened, and Ms. Buckley smiled down at her. "Please come in, Cassie."

Cassie stepped inside, folding the note in half and then in half again. Was she in trouble? She hoped not. She stood just inside the doorway, not quite sure how to ask what was going on.

"Sit down, Cassie." Ms. Buckley sat behind the table with her chin in her hand.

Cassie pulled out a chair and sat on the edge.

"How are you dealing? I heard about your dog."

Oh. That's what this was about. Cassie let out a small

exhale. She tried not to think about Scaredy. Competing in Science Olympiad had helped. The weekend had been harder, but now that she was back in school, she could distract herself. "I think I'm doing okay."

"It's okay to be sad, Cassie. You need to process what you're feeling. The first step of grieving is to not hide it from yourself."

"I don't think I am," she said. "I've cried a lot. It helps when I have something else to focus on."

"That's great." Ms. Buckley swiveled to a file cabinet behind her. "I have something else for you to do, if you're up to it."

"Sure. What is it?"

Ms. Buckley placed a manila folder on the table. "We're starting a buddy program with the special education kids. Some of them need a friend during P.E. and lunch. Maddix Dale requested you to be his buddy. Would you be interested in doing something like that?"

Cassie thought about the dark-haired boy who always smiled and waved at her during P.E. and when he passed her in the hall. She'd gone out of her way to be friendly to him, feeling sorry for him when the other kids teased him because of his weight or the way he talked. "Of course! I would love to."

"Wonderful, Cassie. I knew I could count on you." Ms. Buckey opened the folder and wrote Cassie's name across the top. "I think this will be really good for you, too. It will help take your mind off your dog's death."

Cassie blinked, her eyes warming at the unexpected use

of that word. She swallowed past a sudden lump. "Yeah."

"And sometimes there'll be school events that I'll need your help with. You're one of the friendliest students in school, Cassie. You're smart and you're a leader. I hope you don't mind setting an example for your peers."

Her, a leader? An example to her peers? Ms. Buckley didn't know her that well. "I don't mind. I'll do whatever you need."

♥

Three days later, Cassie got called to the cafeteria to help with an assembly.

"I'm Mr. Mac," the athletic man with a tight blue shirt and a microphone headpiece said to her and the three other kids gathered around him. "We're going to be doing a pep rally for your classmates in preparation of the tests you take next week."

Tests. Ugh. Cassie made a face. She hated taking tests. The other kids groaned, echoing her sentiments.

Mr. Mack grinned. "See? Everyone hates tests. You're all kids in the buddy program, right?"

Cassie nodded along with the others.

"So if you think tests are hard for you, imagine how much harder they must be for someone with a handicap."

Cassie thought about Maddix. It would be so much harder for him to focus on a test. He was easily distracted. He'd probably get so nervous about it that he'd blow it before he started. "So how are we going to help them?"

Mr. Mac snapped his fingers and pointed at her. "That's the golden question. We're going to make a cheer. And then perform it for them."

One of the boys in the group balked. "Like cheerleaders?"

"Yep. Without the short skirts." Mr. Mac beamed.

Making a cheer didn't sound so bad. "Sounds like fun!"

The boy scowled at her, but Mr. Mac said, "All right, let's jam!"

"And peanut butter," Cassie echoed.

Mr. Mac laughed. "Jam and peanut butter. Good one!"

Cassie smiled, pleased with herself.

It only took an hour to come up with their routine. The boys said no climbing and no splits, so the cheer consisted of shouting, clapping, and jumping.

Mr. Mac took them to the patio out back, where they found all of the fifth grade classes sitting on the concrete. The sun stared down from the deep blue sky, the promise of summer wavering around the edges.

Mr. Mac led them in the cheer. "We."

"Are!" the girls shouted.

"The," the boys yelled, with slightly less enthusiasm.

"Testbusters!" they shouted together, following it up with clapping and yelling. Two of the other girls did a high kick into the air, which Cassie didn't even try to imitate.

The whole show only last about fifteen minutes, but the students got involved, standing up and yelling, jumping when they could. The testbusters wove through the crowd and pulled out the special ed kids. Cassie led Maddix to the front, where she helped him lead the group in a cheer. The other students did the same. Mr. Mac gathered them around him when it was over.

"You did awesome, testbusters," he said, giving everyone high fives. "You watch and see how much their confidence increases now. Everyone will nail those tests!"

The fifth grade teachers began lining up their kids to take them inside. Cassie wandered over to Maddix, who stood making weird armpit noises with another kid from special ed. Both laughed hysterically.

"Hey, good job today, Maddix," she said, joining them.

His friend burst out laughing, but Maddix straightened up. "I'm glad I could help. Thank you for asking me, Cassie."

"Sure." Cassie waved at him. "Good luck on your tests next week. I'll see you at the assembly, okay?" The honor roll Assembly was Friday, after the standardized testing days were over.

"Yep." Maddix beamed.

Cassie started to walk away, and laughter burst out behind her. She turned around to see Maddix turning bright red while his friend cuffed him over the head. She shook her head and kept going.

"Testbusters!" Mr. Mac yelled from the front of the patio. "Come back up here, please!"

"What are we doing now?" Cassie asked Jerry Freeman, one of the fellow testbusters.

"How should I know?" Jerry said, rolling his eyes. He moved in front of her, and Cassie scowled. How did someone like him end up as a buddy and a testbuster, anyway?

"Hey, you guys did fantastic," Mr. Mac said, wiping

sweat from his brow. He hadn't even been jumping, and he was sweaty. "Ms. Buckley wants all of you to go back to her office."

"Really?" Kendra Melendez, the other girl, perked up. "We don't have to go back to class?"

He shook his head. "Not today. Today you are home free."

Cassie followed behind as they trooped into the building and down the hall. Even though she'd just spent the afternoon making routines and spending time with these kids, she didn't feel included. None of them had really gone out of their way to talk to her.

Ms. Buckley had a surprise for them: soda.

"No way!" Jerry exclaimed, grabbing a Pepsi. Cassie quickly grabbed the orange one before anyone could get it.

"Thank you for being so helpful today," Ms. Buckley said. "You can go back to class if you want. Or you can stay in here and play games, since you obviously work so well together."

"Games!" Kendra said.

The other three kids argued over Jenga or Uno, but Cassie had a better idea. She spotted a box of dominoes and pulled it out. "Let's make a domino tower!"

They fell silent and looked at her, their expressions blank.

"A domino tower?" Jerry echoed. "Do you even know how to do that?"

"Are you kidding?" Cassie dumped the dominoes on the table. "You mean you don't?"

It must have been the right thing to say. Jerry's eyes

narrowed, and he scooted his chair closer. "I'll show you a domino tower."

The boys took over, setting up an S-shaped domino line. They knocked it over and yelled in triumph. Cassie nodded.

"Yeah, that wasn't bad," she said. "It was also pretty simple, don't you think?" The boys gaped at her, and she stair-stepped the dominoes by placing a single domino upright. In front of it she put another upright domino, but this time she balanced a second on top of it. She put two on top of the next.

Jerry crossed his arms over his chest. "That's going to fall."

"Only when I want it to," she replied.

They watched as Cassie made the S construction again, this time ending with the stair-stepped domino towers. She had five dominoes left over. Squinting and estimating the distance of the fall, she made another row behind the tallest tower. "It's ready," she said, backing away. She pushed the first domino in the S. It hit the next, and the next. . . . They fell succinctly, exactly the way she planned. She only exhaled when the tall tower collapsed, hitting the final row of five.

"That was awesome!" the other boy exclaimed.

"Quite a tower," Kendra echoed.

"Let's do it again," Jerry said, his face aglow with excitement. "But let's add to it."

Cassie sat back, giggling. They'd liked her domino idea.

CHAPTER THIRTY-NINE
Not So Honorable

The only good part to a week of standardized testing was ending it.

"It's over," Ms. Dawson said, handing everyone their journals. "Now we get back to normal schedule. Take the next ten minutes to write about the tests and how they made you feel."

How they made her feel? That had to be a joke of an idea. Was there any student alive that felt anything besides anxiety when the timer started ticking away and the classroom fell dead silent, every student trying to dredge up everything they ever learned about a subject and get it down into properly filled little circles in just forty-five minute time increments?

It took much less than ten minutes for Cassie to write in her journal.

I hate taking tests. It was miserable. I felt sick to my stomach every morning. I'm so glad it's over. I would rather have homework every night than take another test.

There was nothing else she wanted to say on the subject. She kept her pencil poised over the paper, though, lest Ms. Dawson notice that she wasn't writing anymore.

The fuzzy sound that always preceded announcements filled the room, and the class sat to attention.

"Teachers, we'll begin dismissing for the honor roll assembly now. Fifth and sixth graders, please exit though the back of the school and come into the cafeteria from outside."

Cassie jumped into line, claiming her spot behind Riley. "I love the honor roll assembly," Cassie said. "It's like a big announcement that school is almost over."

"That's because you always make honor roll," Riley said grumpily.

Cassie had no response to that. Riley wasn't dumb; she just didn't like to do anything with school. "Maybe you'll make it this time?" she suggested.

"I already know my grades," Riley replied, rolling her eyes.

Cassie was spared from having to make a further response when Ms. Dawson led them from the room. They went out the back of the school and cut around the side.

The younger kids were already in the cafeteria, sitting in long lines on the hard floor. The teachers sat in chairs in the aisles. The noise blasted Cassie's ears when she walked in.

"Fifth graders over here," Ms. Frats, the school principle, said. They filed into a row behind Ms. Wade's class.

As soon as Cassie sat down on the cold linoleum floor,

the chatter began. Becky leaned across her to talk to Andrea, and a kid in front turned around to talk to Mathew. Ms. Dawson huddled up with the other fifth grade teachers, and they began an intense conversation, throwing their arms out and laughing every few moments.

It wasn't Cassie's first assembly, but the noise level shocked her. Somewhere in this crowd were her sister and brother, but she could barely see past the heads in the row in front of her, much less the third and first graders.

The sixth graders filed in, occupying the space behind them and filling up the cafeteria. Only once they had seated did the teachers begin to walk among the kids, fingers to their lips as they shushed them.

Ms. Frats climbed the stage and stopped in front of the microphone. "Welcome, Walker Wildcats, to our honor roll assembly!"

The loud cheering roared through the room like a wave crashing on the shore.

Ms. Frats clapped her hands until everyone quieted down. "Congratulations on completing your standardized tests! With just two more weeks of school, the finish line is in sight!"

This time even the teachers smiled and cheered. Cassie leaned forward to catch Riley's eye, giving her a big smile. *See?* she thought. *That's what this is all about. We're almost done with fifth grade.*

Riley nodded but didn't return the smile.

"To begin," Ms. Frats continued. "We will start with our most dedicated students. When I say your name, please stand. The Walker Whizzes!"

Cassie sat up straighter as Ms. Frats explained that the Walker Whizzes were the kids who had straight As, who managed to average a perfect four-point-oh. She hoped she was in this group. She studied hard, did her homework on time, and always got good grades on her tests.

Ms. Frats began calling out names, starting with the first graders. Easy for them to maintain a high grade. What was hard in first grade? She noticed Scott's name wasn't called, but that wasn't a big shock. He hated school and hated doing his homework.

Ms. Frats had reached third grade now. The group of students standing was small, just a few scattered throughout each class.

"Emily Jones."

Cassie's ears perked up. That was her sister. If her younger sister was a Walker Whiz, she certainly would be, too.

Ms. Frats had reached the fifth graders. She called Emmett's name, then Jerry Freeman. Almost Cassie's turn.

"Cheri Kelsey."

Wait. She'd skipped Cassie! Cassie wanted to jump up and interrupt her, but she knew that it was futile. Her eyes burned and she swallowed past a lump in her throat. A mistake, it had to be a mistake. How could Emily possibly have done better than her?

Ms. Frats moved on to the sixth graders, and Cassie tried hard not to cry. It wasn't a mistake. She hadn't made the honor roll.

"Everyone give a big round of applause for our Walker Whizzes!" The clapping was less enthusiastic this time. "Please be seated. And now for our next group: the Wildcat Wonders!"

Cassie tuned out her voice as Ms. Frats described these students as having mostly As with a few Bs. All she really heard was that these kids weren't as good or as smart as the first group. If she wasn't a Walker Whiz, she may as well be nothing.

The list was longer this time, with many more student standing when Ms. Frats went through the grades. Cassie wasn't surprised when her name was called with several other fifth graders. She stood up, blinking back tears that she hoped no one noticed. She didn't want to be a Wildcat Wonder.

Ms. Frats congratulated them all and Cassie quickly sat down, glad not to be under everyone's gazes anymore. She didn't pay attention to the rest of the assembly.

CHAPTER FORTY

Greenhouse Bombs

Spirits were high as they headed back to class, the kids all riled up and excited. Almost half of the kids had made the honor roll with a three-point-oh or above. Cassie couldn't get over the heavy disappointment in her chest. She really thought she'd done better than that.

"Don't forget your greenhouses!" Ms. Dawson called over the dull roar of students gathering their backpacks. "Sunday is Mother's Day!"

Cassie dutifully went to the window and picked up her plant. It really had grown quite nicely.

"Cassie." Ms. Dawson stopped her as she headed for the door. "You've seemed a bit sad all day. What's wrong?"

"Oh, nothing." She forced a smile. Even she knew she had no reason to be upset. "I'm fine. Ready for the weekend."

"Uh-huh." Ms. Dawson leaned closer. "Is it because of the honor roll?"

Cassie couldn't help it. "I thought I did better than that!" she blurted. "I thought I was doing really well in school."

Ms. Dawson crossed her arms over her chest, but her eyes were gentle. "There's a whole lot more to school than just grades, Cassie. Look what you've done in the past few weeks. You're a part of the buddy program. You were a testbuster. You're accomplishing a lot more than just getting good grades. That's all part of your education, Cassandra."

Cassie considered her words, and then she nodded. "Yeah. You're right." She couldn't quite bring herself to let go of the sadness, but her teacher's words made a lot of sense. She had accomplished a lot this year.

She didn't have time to mull over her honor roll status for long, anyway.

"Cassie," her dad said at dinner, "are you ready for the talent show?"

The talent show. She put her fork down, her stomach rolling up into a knot. She'd kind of forgotten about it, with everything else going on. "When is it, again?"

"Monday night," her mom said. "We'll all be there to watch you."

Monday. The knot in her stomach tightened. That left her just the weekend to prepare. She forced her lips upward into a smile. "It'll be great." It was just a clarinet, after all. How hard could it be? She'd do one of the songs they'd practiced in band.

She practiced all day Saturday.

Her dad came in and sat by her, and Cassie waited for him to tell her that she was doing a good job.

"Tomorrow's Mother's Day," he said instead.

"Oh, I know," Cassie said, brightening. "I have this really cool gift for Mom. It's—"

He interrupted her. "I'm more concerned about my mom. Do you have something for Grandma?"

Grandma. Cassie felt her face drop. She hadn't even thought of her. "I could make her a card." If it sounded lame, it had to sound even worse to her father.

"Your mom and I have talked about this. Why don't you make the card for your mother and give your other gift to Grandma? It would be a nice gesture. Especially after how you were during her last visit."

Cassie hated to admit he had a point. She put the clarinet back in her mouth and returned to practicing.

Mr. Jones left, but his words lingered. Before Cassie went to bed, she made up her mind. She drew a beautiful card for her mother and wrote a four-lined poem inside. Then for her grandmother, she carefully wrapped up her greenhouse plant.

"To Grandma," she wrote on a note. "Because you always take such good care of things."

Satisfied with herself, she went to bed.

Right after church, Mr. Jones left to get Grandma. Cassie could hardly keep down her excitement about her gift, certain her grandmother would love it. She told her mom all about it while they peeled potatoes.

"It was going to be for you, Mom."

"Cassie, that means the world to me. And I'm sure your grandma will appreciate it even more."

Mr. Jones must've had the talk with all the children, because Grandma had an assortment of mishappen gifts placed in front of her as soon as she sat on the couch.

"Happy Mother's Day, Mom," Mr. Jones said, kissing her cheek and handing her a box with an extravagant bow on it.

"Chocolate-covered cherries," Grandma said, opening it. "My favorite." She opened each one in turn, oohing over the cut-out snowflake and ironed magnets.

Finally she got to Cassie's, and Cassie sat up straighter. She couldn't wait for her family to see this.

Grandma picked up the soda-bottle from its upright position on the floor. "A bomb!" she shouted, giving it three good, solid shakes.

Cassie pressed her hands to her cheeks and gasped. "Grandma, no!" she cried.

"Janet," Mrs. Jones murmured, stepping in and taking the bottle from her. "That was fragile."

Cassie wanted to tear her eyes away as her grandmother slowly unwrapped the greenhouse.

The growing little plant was gone. Dirt splattered the sides of the soda-bottle, coating the top. Cassie burst into tears. Giving something that special to her grandmother had been a foolish mistake.

Grandma kept apologizing. Mrs. Jones set the bottle in the kitchen window.

"Maybe it will grow back, Cassie," she said.

"Mine was the best in the class," Cassie murmured bitterly.

Her mother put an arm around her shoulders and kissed

her temple. "I'm sure it was beautiful, Cassie," she whispered. "And someday we'll laugh about this."

CHAPTER FORTY-ONE

Squeaky Nerves

The rest of Mother's Day flew by in a hurry, and before she'd even had a chance to pull out her instrument, it was bed time.

At least thoughts of the impending talent show shortened her greenhouse mourning time. She woke up feeling queasy and shaky, and she knew it wasn't because of a dead plant.

"Get up, Cassie," Emily said, turning on the light and shaking her. "It's time to get ready for school."

"I don't think I can go," she said, pulling the blanket over her head. "My throat hurts." She gave a mild cough.

"I'll get Mom." Emily left the room and Cassie groaned. She might be able to fool her sister, but not her mother.

"Cassie?" Mrs. Jones moved the blanket and peered at Cassie. She pressed a hand to her forehead. "What's wrong?"

"I just don't feel so great," Cassie replied.

"Hmm. You don't have a fever." Her mom went to the closet and retrieved a shirt and pants. "I think you're just nervous for the talent show tonight, honey."

She had that right.

"Get dressed, and we'll see how you feel."

There was no way around it. Cassie dressed quickly, wishing she could stay home and practice all day. She didn't feel prepared for this. She should have been practicing all month, not just one day.

At the end of the school day, Ms. King called for all the kids in the talent show to come to the music room. They would stay and rehearse for an hour before the show officially started.

Cassie put her clarinet together, taking careful breaths. This was it. Now was her chance to warm-up, to make sure her piece was smooth and perfect.

She set up her sheet music just for her warm-up. She had the song memorized, but figured it couldn't hurt to make sure she was doing it correctly. The sight of the two sheets boosted her confidence. It wasn't very long. Surely she could get through this uncomplicated, simple song without messing up.

Cassie pressed the reed between her lips and blew. The note that squeaked out was anything but pleasant. Wincing, Cassie ran through a scale, squinting every time the clarinet squeaked.

"What are you playing there, a mouse?" Conner Lane teased, laughing.

Cassie blinked quickly, hoping her face didn't give away

her dismay. "I just have to warm up."

"Right." He guffawed.

Her hands were shaking now, and she forgot the notes three times in the first run-through. And the clarinet wouldn't stop squeaking. This was not going good.

After running through it two more times, she felt more certain than ever that this would be a horrible disaster. Ms. King came in with a sheet listing the order of appearance. "A parent will come and get you and take you into the wings of the stage. Until then, you can hang out in here, but don't play music. It needs to be quieter."

The students settled into an enthusiastic chatter, but Cassie sat with her hands folded in her lap. She could hardly think, let alone make small talk.

One by one, the kids were called back to perform. Cassie wished she could watch them instead of sit back here feeling sick to her stomach. Her family must be in the audience by now. She picked up her clarinet and gripped it tightly.

The parent poked her head in the room, consulting her paper. "Cassandra Jones?" She lifted her eyes and glanced around.

Cassie stood, her knees quivering. "Here." She followed the woman up the stairs and waited behind the curtains. She didn't pay any attention to the acts before her. All she could imagine was herself, standing on the stage and playing horribly.

The clapping started, and the second grader on the stage walked toward them.

"Your turn," the woman whispered, nudging Cassie onward.

Cassie cleared her throat and forced her feet to move one in front of the other. She reached the microphone and stared out at the darkened cafeteria. At least she couldn't make out any faces. She took a deep breath and spoke.

"My name is Cassandra Jones, and I'm going to play 'When the Saints come Marching in' on my clarinet." She paused, and then added quickly, "And I'm a beginner, so don't laugh at me if I mess up."

That brought some gentle titters from the audience. Cassie lifted the instrument to her mouth and began to play.

Her mind stayed two steps ahead of her fingers, conjuring the music notes from her memory before her hands had to play them. The song finished, and Cassie didn't move. Was it really over? Slowly she pulled the clarinet from her mouth and bowed.

Only then did the crowd in front of her start clapping. Somewhere a man hollered, and she smiled, suspecting it was her father. She couldn't believe it! The clarinet hadn't even squeaked!

She turned and walked off the stage, flush with triumph and confidence. She'd done it, and much better than she'd expected.

♥

The last day of school finally rolled around. Cassie joined her classmates in quizzes and outdoor competitions. Then they lazed around the classroom having chips, candy, and soda, and discussing their summer plans.

"I'll probably spend time with my grandparents in southern Arkansas," Riley said. "That's what I usually do in the summer."

"I'm going to see my grandparents too!" Cassie said. "I don't know them really well. I've never been to their house. But we're all going to Arizona in July to spend a week with them." Her parents had just broken that news to them the night before. Cassie was beyond excited.

"Wow, that's fun!" Riley said. "My brother and I will be going by ourselves."

"Us too!" Cassie beamed.

Riley frowned, one hand pressing down the side of her short hair. "But how will you get to Arizona, then?"

"We're flying."

Her frown deepened. "By yourselves?"

"Yep."

"That doesn't seem very safe."

Ms. Dawson clapped her hands to get everyone's attention.

"Students," she said, "it's been a wonderful year with all of you. Today's your last day of fifth grade. When you step foot in this school again, you'll be sixth graders."

The bell to dismiss car riders rang, and almost everyone stood up, chattering boisterously.

"Have a great summer!" Ms. Dawson yelled over the din.

"You're not riding the bus today?" Riley asked as Cassie gathered up her lunch box and backpack.

She shook her head. "Not today. My mom's picking us

up. Kind of a last-day-of-school celebration thing." She gave a wave and shouldered her backpack, heavy-laden with unused school supplies and projects. "I'll call you when we get back from Arizona!"

Riley lifted a shoulder. "You can try. After I go to my grandparents, I'm going to Girls' club camp for the summer. I might be hard to reach."

"Oh." Cassie paused, momentarily deflated. Then she perked up. "Maybe I'll come to camp too!"

A corner of Riley's lip quirked up. "Maybe."

Riley seemed less than enthusiastic about the idea. Cassie gave another wave and left the classroom, too excited about what the summer was bringing to worry much about Riley.

Get your own Cassandra Jones Season 1 journal to record your very own extraordinary life! Personalize the title to be your book and laugh at excepts from Walker Wildcats Year 1 sprinkled throughout the book. Available now!

The adventure continues with Cassandra Jones in sixth grade! *Walker Wildcats Year 2* available now!

About the Author

Tamara Hart Heiner is a mom, wife, baker, editor, and author. She currently lives in Arkansas with her husband, four children, a cat, a guinea pig, and several fish. She would love to add a macaw and a sugar glider to the family. She's the author of several young adult suspense series as well as a nonfiction book about the Joplin Tornado, *Tornado Warning.*

Join the Cassandra Jones Fan Club online and discover all things Cassandra! Interact with the author, find out secret information, and get sneak peeks into future books!

https://www.facebook.com/groups/
AllAboutCassandraJones

Made in the USA
Middletown, DE
21 July 2020